The Knight of Stars and Storms

Terry Deary was born in Sunderland and now lives in County Durham, where the Marsdens of *Tudor Chronicles* lived. Once an actor, he has also been a teacher of English and drama and has led hundreds of workshops for children in schools. He is the author of the bestselling *Horrible Histories* and of many other successful books for children, both fiction and non-fiction.

Also available

The Prince of Rags and Patches
The King in Blood Red and Gold
The Lady of Fire and Tears

Coming soon

The Lord of the Dreaming Globe
The Queen of the Dying Light

TUDOR CHRONICLES

The Knight of
Stars and Storms

TERRY DEARY

Orion
Children's Books

First published in Great Britain in 1998
as an Orion hardback
and a Dolphin paperback

This new edition published 2005 by
Orion Children's Books
a division of the Orion Publishing Group Ltd
Orion House
5 Upper St Martin's Lane
London WC2H 9EA

A catalogue record for this book is
available from the British Library

Printed in Great Britain by Clays Ltd, St Ives plc

ISBN 1 84255 150 7

www.orionbooks.co.uk

Contents

All chapter titles are quotations from *The Merchant of Venice*. This play was written by William Shakespeare in 1596, the year in which Sir Francis Drake died. It is a play about hatred and revenge.

The Marsden Family

WILLIAM MARSDEN *The narrator*
The youngest member of the family. Training to be a knight as his ancestors were before him, although the great days of knighthood are long gone. His father insists on it and Great-Uncle George hopes for it. But he'd rather be an actor like the travelling players he has seen in the city. He can dream.

Grandmother **LADY ELEANOR MARSDEN**
She was a lady-in-waiting to Queen Anne Boleyn. After seeing the fate of her mistress she came to hate all men, she married one, maybe out of revenge. Behind her sharp tongue there is a sharper brain. She is wiser than she looks.

Grandfather **SIR CLIFFORD MARSDEN**
He was a soldier in Henry VIII's army where (Grandmother says) the batterings softened his brain. Sir Clifford is the head of the family although he does not manage the estate these days he simply looks after the money it makes. He is well known for throwing his gold around like an armless man.

Great-Uncle SIR GEORGE SULGRAVE
A knight who lost his lands and now lives with his stepsister, Grandmother Marsden. He lives in the past and enjoys fifty-year-old stories as much as he enjoys fifty-year-old wine. He never lets the truth stand in the way of a good story.

SIR JAMES MARSDEN *William's father*
He runs the Marsden estate and is magistrate for the district. He believes that, without him, the forces of evil would take over the whole of the land. This makes him a harsh and humourless judge. As a result he is as popular as the plague.

LADY MARSDEN *William's mother*
She was a lady-in-waiting to Mary Queen of Scots. Then she married Sir James. No one quite knows why. She is beautiful, intelligent, caring and witty. Quite the opposite of her husband and everyone else in the house.

MARGARET "MEG" LUMLEY
Not a member of the family, but needs to be included for she seems to be involved in all the family tales. A poor peasant and serving girl, but bright, fearless and honest (she says). Also beautiful under her weather-stained skin and the most loyal friend any family could wish for (she says).

CHAPTER ONE

"Thou know'st that all my fortunes are at sea"

The road is little more than a grassy track that runs along the side of the river. There are two deep ruts that are filled with mud in the winter and dust in the summer. That's where the wagons were dragged along by sweating horses till they reached the mouth of the river and the ships.

Not many people use the road now. To a stranger it looks like any other lonely track. But, to me, it is something more. It is the road that leads back home.

I know every foot of the road. It winds under the shadow of Penshaw Hill until it reaches Fatfield Bridge. Once it has crossed the bridge, the road rises and you can see the towers of an ancient house rising above the trees. That's the first sight of Marsden Hall. My home.

When I was a boy, in the last days of the great Queen Elizabeth, I rode that path on my blue roan mare many times, yet I never grew tired of the thrill that first sight of Marsden Hall gave me. It seemed that the house, inside its high stone wall, had been there as long as the distant hills and the river. I never imagined it could vanish. I couldn't picture Marsden Hall without my family living there, as they had done for two hundred years or more. But I was young and I didn't understand how easily these things can happen.

I learned to understand that summer, that disastrous summer of storms and ruin. And it was like a summer storm; the sort of storm where clouds suddenly appear in a clear sky, cover the sun and lash unlucky travellers with freezing rain.

The sky was blue that day when it all started – and the Marsden family were the unlucky travellers on that road from the river mouth back to Marsden Hall.

We took one last look at the ships in Wearmouth Harbour with sun-browned workers loading and unloading them. Bales of wool were hoisted on wooden ropes and pulleys and lowered into the deep holds of the ships at the quayside.

Coal wagons ran on wooden rails to the edge of the docks and tipped their filthy loads while sailors on the decks repaired sails and ropes.

Then we strained our eyes to the horizon where our ship, the *Pelican II*, was disappearing into a haze. "God speed!" my father cried, waving his hat as if the crew could see or hear him. It was unusual to see my father's sour face suddenly so full of life and excitement. It was a thin, pinched face with close-set eyes that always looked suspicious. He turned to me. "She'll make our fortune, Will."

"Yes, Father," I said.

"Grandmother will have dinner ready for us, James," my mother said with a gentle smile. "We should be getting back to Marsden Hall."

"Of course. But it's worth being late for dinner on a great occasion like this," Father said.

My mother bowed her head in silent agreement and turned her horse towards home, about eight miles upriver from the port.

My grandfather rode at the head of the group, as he always did. He was so old he could remember Elizabeth's monstrous father, King Henry VIII, but age hadn't dimmed his sharp brain. He rode alongside his stepbrother-in-law, my Great-Uncle George, the old knight with the flowing white beard, who loved life as he loved old wine, and drank both with a huge thirst.

My mother rode next to her maid, Meg. The girl was an orphan and my father had wanted to put her in the almshouse. Mother had persuaded him to give her a job as a serving maid, and she had proved so valuable that Mother had made Meg her personal servant. Meg's old clothes had been replaced with new ones and her wild chestnut hair had been tamed. Her fierce spirit was as strong as ever. She ought to have paid me some respect, as the son of her mistress; she treated me more like a brother. By now I had realized she'd never change. And I had begun to understand I didn't want her to.

The twin wheel-ruts on the road made it natural for us to ride in pairs and Meg fell in alongside Mother. I was left to ride with my father, never the most cheerful way to spend an hour.

But that day he was eager to talk and to explain. For once he wasn't talking about his duties as a magistrate and the punishments he'd dealt to the wretched and shabby criminals in our district. He wanted to talk about his hopes for the Marsden estate, and for once I wanted to listen.

"We've lived comfortably at Marsden, I know. But when that ship has made a few journeys, we'll be rich, William. Rich!"

"Yes, Father."

"For years we've taken coal out of our pit at Sulgrave

and sold it to London. But where has all the profit gone, Will? Can you tell me that?"

"To the shipowners," I replied. I knew this because I'd heard some of the arguments that he'd had with my grandfather over the cost of building our own ships.

"Exactly! But now we own the *Pelican II*, it only costs me the crew's wages and all the profit from the coal comes to *us*. We should have had our own ships built years ago, William! Years ago!"

"But Grandfather wouldn't allow it."

He sighed. "Old people can be very set in their ways. I was going to wait till he died, then go ahead. But it seems as if he'll live forever!"

My father sounded almost disappointed at the thought.

"Grandfather was worried about the ship sinking," I reminded my father.

"And that's why I'm having *new* ships built, Will. I'm not buying some worm-eaten old hulk that's past its best. No, the *Pelican II* is built of finest oak from our own Bournmoor Woods – and she is unsinkable. You must remember, Will, I know more about ships than any man in England. Unsinkable, believe me."

"Yes, Father."

When we reached Southwick, Father pointed across the river. "Look, William, over there! That ship that's almost finished. That's the *Hawk*. Our second ship."

"You pointed it out on the journey down," I said.

"So I did, so I did. When that's sailing, we'll be twice as rich. Of course I'll need help to control the Marsden estate. I can't be magistrate and landlord and mine-owner and shipowner all on my own, and your grandfather's getting too old to help now. That's why I expect you to take over some of my duties."

I had mentioned once before that I wanted to go to London to join a theatre company. The idea had made my father explode with rage. Now I simply said, "What about my lessons?"

"What? Your Latin? You know enough to study a little law. So, you can give up lessons after harvest time this year and start doing the estate accounts while I look after our shipping business."

The thought of spending my days in Father's dreary room with account books almost made me sick.

The sun passed behind a cloud and a breeze from the coast chilled me. Maybe it was the thought of the living death that lay ahead of me.

Great-Uncle George stopped and looked up at the sky. "We'll be soaked before we reach Marsden Hall," he called to us, kicking his horse into a quick trot.

Father's good mood vanished with the sun. "What's wrong?" I asked him.

"That wind. It's turned to the east. It'll be driving the *Pelican II* back on to the coast. She'll be at about Hartlepool by now. Dangerous rocks there. I hope Captain Walsh knows what he's doing."

"You hired him," I said.

"I had very little choice," Father snapped, back to his usual sour voice. "The best captains are already employed on other ships. I had to take what I could get."

"You could have offered more money to one of the good captains," I suggested. It was the wrong thing to say. As large spots of rain slapped the back of my neck, Father's storm began to break.

"Don't tell me my business, boy. Captain Walsh was cheap. The less we pay the crew the more profit we make."

"Not if he costs us a ship," I thought. I had enough sense to keep my mouth shut and hurry after the rest of the family. Father spurred on his horse savagely and left me behind.

The rain fell so heavily it swamped the path and began to bounce in the puddles. The horses kicked up the mud and spattered the riders at the back. We skidded over the planks of Fatfield Bridge and climbed away from the edge of the river. The rain ran into my eyes, but I could just make out the towers of Marsden Hall, solid and welcoming as ever. I ducked my head and rode hard.

As Great-Uncle George had predicted, we were soaked by the time we reached home. Meg and I took the horses while the others went inside to dry themselves. She was cheerful in spite of the soaking. "Were you excited? Seeing your first ship sail off like that?"

"It's a collier full of coal," I said. "It's not a treasure ship."

"Have you been stung by a bee?" she asked.

"No. Why?"

"I just wondered what put you in such a bad mood."

I sighed. "Father plans to make me help with managing the estate. I'll never get to London."

Meg nodded. She knew how much my dream meant to me. "Take a ship."

"Steal it?"

"No, Will. When the *Pelican II* returns, you can offer to sail with it on the next voyage to London. Say you want to see how the shipping business works. Then, when you get to London, 'forget' to come back home!"

"Meg!" I cried. "That's . . . that's deception. Are you suggesting I should lie to my father?"

"Yes."

I scowled at her. "That's wicked."

She grinned back. "But it's a good idea, isn't it?"

"Yes," I said, as I handed the horses to Martin, our ostler, to lead into the stables at the back of the hall.

As Meg and I walked back to the house, she asked, "How does your father know so much about ships? I thought I heard him say he knows more about them than anyone in England. Was that just another one of his tales?"

The sun had come out again, but the wind from the sea was still strong and cool. I shivered. "He sailed with Sir Francis Drake," I told her.

Meg stopped at the side door to the house. "Your father? Sailed with Drake? I didn't know that."

"He doesn't talk about it much," I said.

"Drake was a hero!" she cried.

"Drake was a pirate," I said. "I think my father's a little ashamed of what he did when he sailed with him. After all, Father's the local magistrate. His job is to uphold the law. It would never do for local people to know he went round the world stealing Spanish silver. He'd lose their respect."

Meg laughed. "I think they'd give him *more* respect if they knew."

"Perhaps," I said, stepping into the cool, dim hallway. "But that's not what Father believes."

I walked towards the main hall, but Meg snatched at my sleeve. "Will! Get him to tell us about it."

I knew what she meant. The Marsden family had an old custom. Every evening after supper, we would take it in turns to entertain the rest of the family with a story. Great-Uncle George enjoyed his tales of ancient battles while Grandfather told us about the court of Henry VIII. Father always loved telling us about the crimes he'd uncovered and the villains he'd punished. I agreed with Meg that it would be good to know more about the famous Sir Francis Drake.

"I'll see what I can do," I promised.

I knew that my father would take little notice of my request, so I went to find Grandfather in his room. He would persuade Father to tell us the story.

As usual Grandfather was quarrelling with Grandmother. "Riding to Wearmouth at your age! You ought to know better," she was saying.

"I am not a child, Eleanor."

"I know. A child would have more sense. Now sit still while I dry your hair with this cloth."

He muttered something under his breath, but sat still in the chair while she rubbed at his head a little harder than she needed. "Hello, Will," he said. "Your grandmother is trying to rub the hair off my head because she likes bald men."

"I am trying to rub the hair off his head because it may make it easier for my words to sink through his thick skull. Tell him he's too old to go out riding in the rain."

"You're too old to go out riding in the rain," I said obediently.

"It wasn't raining when we went out," said Grandfather, "and my son James told me it wouldn't rain."

"Take off your clothes," Grandmother ordered.

He groaned, but obeyed. His thin body was pale and shrunken and streaked with purple veins, the skin hanging in folds as if it were meant to fit a larger body. Without clothes he looked older and as frail as a moth's wing. I had a sudden fear that he was close to death.

"Were you pleased with our mighty galleon?" he asked.

I nodded. "Why were you against Father building the ship?" I asked.

Grandmother passed him a fresh white linen shirt and he pulled it over his head. "I think the ships are a good idea. The trouble is we can't *afford* them. We've had a lot of bad harvests in the past few years and some of the coal seams have been poor. Marsden Manor can't afford three thousand pounds for two colliers."

"So how are we buying them?"

"Your father has borrowed the money. There's a coal-owner called Glub in Newcastle. He loaned father the money and we'll have to pay it back from the profits."

"But when they're paid for, we'll be rich," I said.

Grandfather sat down heavily and began to pull his hose up his legs. "If God is good," he muttered.

"And if God isn't good?"

"Then Master Glub will want something in return for his three thousand pounds," Grandfather said.

"What do we have that's worth that amount of money?" I asked.

Grandfather looked at Grandmother. Her wrinkled face was set in hard lines. She gave a flicker of her eyelids. It was a sign for him to go on. "We have Marsden Hall," he said. "This house."

He stood up and slipped on a doubtlet, began lacing it to his breeches. "You have seen horse races by the river in Durham city, Will?" I nodded. "People bet money that their horse will win. Your father is betting with our home."

Grandmother rested a hand on his arm. "We aren't for this world much longer," she said grimly. "It's *your* home, my boy. We're not worried for ourselves. It's your future."

I stood silently and worked it out for a minute. "I could be rich."

"You could be homeless and poor."

I tried to smile. Marsden Hall would never leave the

family. I would always live there, I thought. I'd go away to London, but Marsden would be there whenever I was ready to return. That was certain. There was only one thing more certain. `The *Pelican II* is unsinkable," I said. "My father said so."

There was a faint smile on Grandfather's lips. "And your father said it wouldn't rain."

CHAPTER TWO

"Haste away, for we must measure twenty miles this day"

By the time we had finished supper the summer storms had blown away and it was a fine, warm evening. We went out into the garden to enjoy the last of the daylight.

The steward covered the turf seats with canvas as they were still damp. The rain had freshened the flowers and the roses over the arched walkway were giving off a powerful scent. Those are the days you want to last forever; where you want no one to grow old and die, where you want nothing to change.

Before the evening ended the world had turned upside down, of course. That's the way life does things to you.

My father's good mood had returned and Grandfather had little trouble in persuading him to tell us about his adventures with Francis Drake. "Come along, James," he said, "you boast about your knowledge of the sea, but you're very shy about telling us what you got up to."

My father spread his hands. "You know most of it," he said.

"But your son Will doesn't," my mother put in. "I'm sure he thinks you're a dull old magistrate, who never knew what it was like to be a young adventurer. Isn't that right, Will?" she asked wickedly.

"Yes," I said. "I mean . . . no!"

Meg's sea-green eyes sparkled in delight when she saw my confusion and even Grandmother hid a grin behind her hand. Father didn't seem to notice.

He tried to look modest. "Oh, very well, if you insist," he said. Then he looked round the family group, seated on the horseshoe of turf benches, and added, "But I do hope you will spare me any interruptions."

We nodded and muttered agreement. Father leaned forward and began his tale . . .

SIR JAMES MARSDEN'S STORY

I am not a vain man, you understand. When I tell my story it may seem that I had very little to do with the great events that took place. The truth is I am just being modest.

Of course it was always my ambition to go to sea and explore the world before I settled down to manage Marsden Manor estate. It was *always* my ambition. When it happened, my trip around the world was not planned. But that does not mean I didn't *want* to go. Sometimes accidents happen and a bold man will make the most of them. That's what I did.

I'd never been away from Durham much. Travelling made me ill and, anyway, I had all I needed here in Marsden Manor. I was a lonely child – my brothers and sisters had died in childhood, leaving me to carry the hopes and dreams of my parents. And I never wanted to mix with the rough village boys like Michael the Taverner's son, or the sly, sneaking Wat Grey. They threw mud at me when I walked through the village, but I ignored them and pretended not to care.

I have to say it came as a surprise when my father called me one day and said he wanted me to leave home and "see a bit of life", as he put it.

"Don't you want me here?" I asked him.

"Of course we *want* you," he said, "but you need to learn a little about the world outside Marsden Manor. It will make you a better owner of these estates when I retire – or die."

"But I've learned how to keep the accounts," I said. "I can do them on my own. My tutor always said I have the finest mind for arithmetic and geometry that he had ever known."

That's when my father said something that I didn't understand. Indeed, it was some years before I understood it. He said, "Marsden Manor is not measured in harvests and acres or rents or tons of coal."

"But that's how you've always taught me to measure it."

My father didn't seem to hear me. He went on, "Marsden Manor is the *people* who live here. From the owners, like you and me, to the workers in the fields and pits and workshops. Do you understand, James?"

"Yes, sir," I said. Of course I was lying. I didn't understand. How can a manor be made up of people? It is clearly made up of land and buildings. But I never forgot his words.

"And you need to leave Marsden for a while to meet people, and to try to understand them."

"Where are you sending me?"

"To London."

"It's a long and rough road, sir. There are footpads and outlaws and cutthroats along every foot of the way," I reminded him.

He smiled. "That's why I'm not sending you by land. I'm sending you by sea."

"Oh," I said, "but there are storms and pirates and dangerous currents at sea. And I can't swim."

"Not many sailors *can* swim," said my father. "They believe God will protect them. If they learn how to swim, He will be angry and throw them into the sea."

"I may be seasick," I pointed out.

"Then lean over the side of the ship and vomit, my lad. You leave tomorrow."

I think my mouth may have been a little too dry to reply. It's not that I was afraid, you understand. Just . . . surprised.

My father walked to the door of the hall and called, "Geordie!" A man stepped in from the hallway where he'd been waiting and my father introduced us. "This is my son, James. James, this is Captain Geordie Milburn of the trading ship, the *Swan*."

"I'm pleased to meet you, Captain," I said.

"Call me Geordie," he replied. He was about my age and looked too young to be in command of a ship. He was tall and broad, but there was no fat on him. He had black hair pulled back from his face and tarred into a pigtail at his neck. His teeth were white and strong with no sign of rottenness, apart from one at the side that must have been knocked out. Despite his plain clothes, he was the finest-looking man I had ever seen. His open honest face was one I felt I could trust.

"What is your plan, Geordie?" I asked, offering him my hand. His grip was like the wooden vice some village boys had once trapped my hand in for sport.

"We sail for London tomorrow morning on the tide just before noon. Can you be at Wearmouth Harbour by then?

We're moored at the end of Low Street on the south bank."

If I'd been uncertain about my trip before, the sight of Geordie Milburn and the feel of his capable hand put my mind at rest. I did not sleep that night, but it wasn't from fear so much as eagerness to set sail. My father rode with me to Wearmouth so he could return with my horse. First he gave me instructions about selling our coal and fleeces when I arrived in London. Then he began to give me advice.

My father had lots of good advice. It's not that I ignored it. There was simply so much to learn in that short time I did not take it all in. "Never take your hand off your purse when you're in London – always carry your knife, but never be the first to draw it – help the unfortunate in every way you can, but never give to beggars – beware of women whose words are sweet as honey – keep away from playhouses and bear-baiting pits."

I was dizzy by the time we had reached Wearmouth, dismounted and walked down Low Street to the river's edge. The noise was tremendous. There was singing from the taverns and the shouting of dock workers, the rattling of carts and the groaning of the ships as they rolled in the river swell. And there was the screaming of the gulls over a fishing boat that was landing its catch.

"If the gulls are out, good luck's about," my father said suddenly.

"Is that true?"

"I don't know. It's what your grandfather used to say. I was a child when he died at the Battle of Flodden Field, but I still remember some of the things he used to say."

"What else did he say?" I asked.

"Red sky at night, sailors delight; red sky in morning, sailors take warning."

"Why should they do that, sir?" I asked.

"Something about storms, I think."

I tried to remember what colour the sky had been that morning. We took some leather bags with clean linen and spare clothes. There was gold stowed at the bottom of the bag, if I should need it, and a bottle of mysterious yellow liquid that my father had slipped in before I left. As I walked up the dangerous plank from shore to ship I asked him, "What is the liquid for?"

"It's a mixture made up by an old friend of mine, Jane Atkinson."

"The village witch?"

"The village wise woman," he said, correcting me. "She says it will protect you from the dreadful sailor's disease they call scurvy."

"It sounds dreadful," I said. I hurried along the plank before I could fall into the dark water below.

"Nothing to worry about, son. Your skin dries up, then your joints start to ache and you grow weaker. Your gums bleed and your teeth drop out – if you don't die first."

"And that's nothing to worry about, sir!"

"Not on the North Sea run. It's only sailors who cross the oceans who suffer from scurvy."

"So why did Mistress Atkinson give you the cordial?"

"Oh, some foolish idea that you would need it before you get back to Marsden. She cast your horoscope and saw a long journey ahead of you. It's probably just foolish nonsense. But take a thimbleful each day and you should stay healthy."

"I think I feel a little sick."

"You can't. You haven't left the dock yet."

He slapped me on the back, walked back down the gangplank and off up Low Street. I was looking forward to seeing him in three weeks' time. If I'd known it was going to be three years I might have run after him!

Geordie Milburn did his best to comfort me on that journey. The waves were as high as a house but he told me it was a calm day and an easy ride for my first sea trip. It was hard to answer him – my breakfast had parted from my stomach before we left the river mouth and last night's dinner was trying to follow it as we ran down the Durham coast.

Then Geordie brought out some instruments and charts on to the deck and began working with them. I could not help but be interested. Geometry has always fascinated me, and Geordie was plotting lines and angles on the chart like the diagrams I used to draw in my schoolroom.

He took out a brass ring and held it up to the sun. "What's that, Geordie?" I asked.

"An astrolabe. It calculates the angle from the ship to the sun. If we know the time of day we can work out how far north we are." He had an hourglass beside him and turned it every time it emptied. It had to be turned every half hour. For the next hour he explained the astrolabe to me and, I have to say, I learned how to use it very quickly. I began charting our trip on the map.

"How do we tell how far east or west we are?" I asked him.

"We have to go by the speed of the ship," he said.

I looked at the swelling grey ocean round us. I knew we were going up and down, but I had no idea how quickly we were going forward. "How on earth do you know that?" I asked him.

He picked up a piece of wood on a rope, strode to the front of the ship and threw the wood into the water. As the ship surged forward the wood seemed to move backwards. We followed the wood to the back of the ship, counting off seconds as we went. "There you are, James!" he said with a grin. "You know the length of the ship, you know how long it took the wood to travel that length. You can work out the speed from that."

It was exactly the sort of arithmetic I enjoyed. I finished the sum in less than five minutes and Geordie was impressed.

All afternoon we ploughed south past the Yorkshire coast, coming in sight of land long enough to check landmarks. By evening I was an expert on the charts. As night fell I could make out the glowing light from a distant town. "That must be Whitby," I said.

Geordie slapped my back and said I was a genius. I felt some pride, although I am naturally a modest man. When the ship's cook served us some stewed lamb from the galley – that's what the ship's kitchen is called – I ate it with a hearty appetite.

I went back to navigation and learned how to plot our position from the Pole Star after sunset. It was all Captain Milburn could do to persuade me to go to my hammock and sleep.

My maths skills had always been useful for working on the estate accounts. But this was different and exciting. By the time we reached London, Geordie had passed over the job of navigation to me while he took care of carpentry work needed to improve the ship. As we sailed into the Thames, he called me a "master mariner" and I thought my heart would burst with pride – although I am a very modest man.

London, twenty-five years ago, was a wild and dangerous place. It was pleasant enough by daylight, I suppose. The streets were crowded with people of every kind. The narrow, dark streets were sometimes so full that you couldn't push your way through. It seemed the taverns never closed and you stumbled over a beggar with every step.

The smell was quite dreadful. There was a law against leaving waste on the streets, but many butchers ignored it. The dogs and flies made short work of the refuse, of course, but the smell lingered on. And without rainfall there was nothing to wash the streets.

Geordie Milburn guided me to the offices of the coal dealers and I made a very good bargain with the Marsden coal we'd carried with us. I was determined not to take the first offer I had for our load. The merchant was almost in tears by the time I had finished dealing with him. "It's warm weather!" he cried.

"I had noticed, sir," I said. "What's that to me?"

"No one needs coal! The price is as low as it gets right now."

I looked towards the city roof tops where the chimneys were spewing out clouds of grey muck that was falling in great black flakes on to the heads of the people in the streets. "Someone is burning coal," I said. "I'll sell my load to them."

"You're a hard man, Master Marsden."

"Hard, but fair," I told him.

"I will give you your price, but don't come back next month. I'll be a ruined man. I'll be in a debtor's prison, you just see if I'm not."

I almost felt sorry for him and lowered the price by a few pence a ton. But in the end he paid me a fair price. "I can only store it till the cold weather comes and hope we have a bitter winter," he groaned.

When I left him my purse was full of silver and my heart full of pride. Geordie told me I'd make a good master of the Marsden estate.

"Will you be celebrating with a little drink in the tavern, James?" he asked.

"I may have a small glass of ale," I said. "Not spirits. Spirits make my brain ache and my legs weak."

"There's a tavern by London Bridge called The Fleece. A lot of sailors meet there. A skilled mariner like you would feel at home there."

"Do you think so?" I asked.

"It's certain."

We headed upriver past the dreadful Tower of London. It was growing dark by the time we reached the tavern. A small wooden picture of a sheep hung over the door, but the place looked more like a small house than a tavern.

Inside it was hot and filled with tobacco smoke, but it was quieter than our own Black Bull Tavern, here in Marsden. Groups of men sat round tables, but kept their heads close together and spoke in murmurs. They stopped talking altogether when we walked past and found a seat in the corner.

A girl with a greasy leather apron over a stained blue dress served us some pleasant fish stew and some strong, dark ale. Then a man came and sat opposite us at the table. He was dressed in plain clothes, although they seemed of fine quality. He had a neat dark beard and eyes brighter than a bird's. "Good evening, Captain Milburn," he said.

The stranger's voice had a strong accent and I found it hard to understand him at first.

"Good evening, Captain Drake," Geordie said.

And that was the first time I ever met Captain Francis Drake.

CHAPTER THREE

"What harm a wind too great might do at sea"

My grandfather sat up stiffly on the turf seat and reached for a flagon of wine that Meg had brought out from the kitchen. "You make me sound a harsh father, James. Packing you off to sea like that."

"I'm sorry, Father. At the time I didn't understand why you made me leave Marsden Manor. But you were quite right. Everyone has to go away some time." He turned to me. "One day you'll go away, William, and it'll do you good to see more of the world."

"Perhaps I could go now," I suggested.

My father's thin face sharpened. "No, William. Not while there is all this extra work to do. When both our ships are working, and earning our fortune, then we can pay someone to keep our accounts. You can make a visit to London – for a week at the most."

I knew that if he didn't let me leave soon, I'd have to run away, but I didn't argue. I smiled and asked, "But you weren't away for a week, were you, Father?"

In the quiet garden there was only the droning sound of some bees gathering the last nectar of the day. Beyond the high walls the sun had set, but the sky was still a bright blue. No one wanted to go indoors yet.

"It's true. I was away rather longer than I intended."

"Longer than *I* intended, too!" Grandfather said suddenly, giving a sharp laugh. "How on earth you managed it I will never understand!"

"I've told you how it happened," Father replied quietly.

"Oh, you've told us!" Great-Uncle George said and he gave a great laugh. "Ha! But if you tell us a hundred times, we still don't understand!"

"It was not a matter for laughter twenty-five years ago," my father said.

"Tell us again, son," Grandmother urged him.

My father looked at me, his narrow eyes holding some kind of warning. "It was a perfectly simply misunderstanding, William. It could have happened to anyone."

"Yes, Father."

He went on with his story. Even the bees seemed to soften their buzzing to listen . . .

SIR JAMES MARSDEN'S STORY

Everyone had heard of Francis Drake. But I was so surprised to come across him in that dark tavern that I spoke a little clumsily. "Francis Drake!" I cried. "The pirate?"

There was a sudden silence as everyone in the tavern stopped their murmured conversations and turned towards me. I was embarrassed and looked at Captain Drake with horror. He had a small red mouth beneath his fair beard. The mouth seemed amused rather than angry. "Your name?" he asked.

"James Marsden of Durham," I said.

"And the finest navigator ever to set foot on the deck of a ship," Geordie said, slapping my back.

"A navigator, eh? A man after my own heart. I am pleased to meet a friend of Geordie Milburn," he said.

Geordie sat back easily on the bench and watched us. "I'm sorry," I stammered, "about the pirate remark. I have heard a lot about you and your brave deeds against the Spanish."

"The Spanish call me pirate," he said calmly. "They also call me dragon and witch. But I think of myself as a knight. The great days of knights on horseback are gone. I am a knight of the sea, and my horse is a ship. I steer by the stars and am driven by the storms. I am a knight of the stars and storms, James."

"Of course, Captain Drake. I meant no offence."

"And I am not offended. You called me a thief? But God himself said, '*I will come on thee as a thief.*'"

"You know your Bible, Captain Drake," I said, surprised.

"My father was a clergyman. He taught us to read using a Bible," Drake said. "I spend three hours of every day in prayer – except when the Spanish guns need my attention."

"'*The prayer of the upright is His delight,*'" I said.

Drake bowed his head graciously and said, "Proverbs fifteen, verse eight." He turned to the pot girl, and ordered a pot of ale and six bottles of Canary wine. "I'm fond of Canary wine," he explained. "It reminds me of the time back in '72 when I led a raid on the Spanish treasure stores at Nombre de Dios north of Panama. It was just a little too daring, I suppose. A tiny band of English sailors against the might of the Spanish army. But we gave them a scare! Ha! That was an attack they will never forget!"

"Your fame has even reached County Durham," I said warmly. I did not say that some travellers reported it was a badly organized and stupid attack. The Spanish army was miles away and Drake was driven off by a few armed citizens of the town.

"If I hadn't been wounded in the leg, we would probably have filled two galleons with the silver and gold and those jewels," he said sadly. "But as we sailed away from Nombre de Dios we captured a Spanish ship, full of Canary wine. I'll swear the two days we spent resting and drinking saved my life. I've been fond of the stuff ever since."

The pot girl brought us the six bottles and Drake pulled the stopper from one and filled a goblet to the brim. He threw the dregs of ale from my own pot and filled it full of wine, opened a second bottle and filled Geordie's pot too. It looked as if we were going to drink two bottles of wine each!

Drake raised his goblet, stood up, looked around the room and said, "Here's to the health of Her Majesty Queen Elizabeth. God bless her and keep her safe."

There were murmurs of "Queen Elizabeth! God bless her!"

I sipped at my wine, but Drake said, "A health is not a health if there is anything left in the cup."

I took a deep breath and swallowed the full mug of wine, half a bottle I'd guess, in one gulp. Drake filled it to the brim again and this time allowed me to sip it a little more slowly.

After that my memory is not so clear, but, remember, it was twenty-five years ago. I *do* know that Drake seemed to take a liking to me straight away, and he let me into a great secret. Not a bit of tavern gossip, or a dockside tale.

A real secret. A great state secret of the Queen herself.

We put our heads together over the wine bottles and Drake said, "Thank you for coming, Geordie."

I remember being a little surprised. I hadn't known that my captain had arranged to meet Drake there. Still, it didn't seem to matter. The great man, Drake himself, liked me and I was proud to be part of his plan.

"The Queen called me to her last month," Drake went on. "She has given me the secret task of raiding some Spanish colonies. I am to take five ships, and a hundred and sixty-four men, and attack the Spanish in their ports on the Pacific coast."

"The Specific!" I cried.

Drake put a finger to his lips. "Hush, Marsden. Spanish spies are everywhere. Queen Elizabeth has sworn on her crown that she will take the head off any man who betrays her secret plan. And we are not going to the Specific coast – we are going to the Pacific coast."

"That's what I said," I told him.

"I think the Canary wine has knotted your northern tongue, my friend. You said 'Specific'. But never mind."

"But no Englishman has ever seen the Pacific Ocean," I said.

"I have seen it," Drake said. "I have stood on a mountain near Panama and looked east to see the Atlantic and west to see the Pacific. I was the first."

"Sorry, Captain Drake," I said. "What I meant to say was, no Englishman has ever sailed from the Atlantic into the Pacific."

Instead he said, "Then I'll be proud to be the first."

"Good luck!" I said, and drank another pot of Canary wine to wish him well.

"I have just one problem. One of the ships that was

joining me from Plymouth struck the Goodwin Sands off the south-east coast. She's too badly damaged to join us. I need another ship and I need it now. You have a ship, Captain Milburn. Is it free?"

"It's being unloaded now," Geordie told him. "I'll have an empty ship tomorrow morning."

"Come with us and you will have a share in the Spanish treasure. You'll be able to buy twenty ships when you return. The thing is," Drake said in a whisper, "we will need to fill her with supplies. You need someone with a hundred pounds in cash to provide all the food and weapons and spare sails that you are going to need."

"I've got a hundred pounds," I said suddenly.

"You have?"

"He has," Geordie agreed. "He's just sold a full cargo of coal."

"Give that hundred pounds to your friend, Captain Milburn, and he'll return in less than two years with ten *thousand* pounds in Spanish treasure."

My mouth went dry at the thought. I went to sup some wine, but my pot was empty. Drake filled it again. "Ten thousand?"

"Ten thousand. Think of what you can do with ten thousands pounds, Marsden."

I fumbled at my belt and pulled out my purse. I pushed it over the table to Geordie. "How will I get home?" I asked him suddenly.

"I'll put you aboard a collier heading for Wearmouth tomorrow," Geordie promised. "Finish your wine," he said. "We'll get back to the *Swan* now. It'll be an early start."

I drained my mug and rose to my feet. The room seemed to be moving like the deck of a ship. They do say this happens when you have been at sea for a few days and come back to dry land. I leaned on Geordie as we walked back down the riverside to where the *Swan* was docked. Torches burned on the battlements of the Tower and its ravens shone black as Durham coal in the flickering light.

The gangplank up to the ship was moving dangerously, but Geordie held me tight and guided me across. I tried climbing into my hammock, but everything was moving too much. The captain let me down on to the floor, threw a cloak over me and said, "You'll be safer there. I'm off to get the supplies we need. I'll see you in the morning."

And I fell into a deep sleep. I seem to remember that I dreamed of sailing across the Atlantic Ocean under the stars and guiding the great Captain Drake to a chest full of Spanish treasure. But when I tried to plunge my hands into the treasure, the gold turned to snakes that wrapped themselves around my arms. I had many wild and frightening dreams that night. It must have been something in The Fleece's fish stew.

I awoke feeling exhausted and ill. The ship was rolling as badly as if she were at sea. I hadn't sailed very often, but I knew she should be steadier than this in the shelter of a London dock.

I could hear sheep bleating in the hold: that had been the sound that woke me. It took me five minutes to get my legs to hold my weight and another five minutes to reach the cabin door since the floor was moving and kept throwing me against the wooden walls.

As well as sheep, I could hear mighty groans that I knew were the ship's timbers twisting under the force of the sea, and the crashing of waves breaking over the side. I opened the door to the smell of tar, mingled with the tang of salt water, and I knew something had gone terribly wrong.

My first aim was to find Geordie Milburn and ask if he'd

changed his mind and decided to sail back to the north. But an even more urgent matter was a trip to the side of the ship to be very sick. That fish stew must have been really bad, I decided. When I finally raised my head, I could make out a blurred green smudge in the distance that was land. I turned, the bitter taste still in my mouth, and headed towards the stern where I expected to find the captain.

Captain Milburn *was* there, wrapped in a heavy cloak against the bitter wind. But I was surprised to see the smiling face of Francis Drake alongside him. He had a long white clay pipe in his mouth and the breeze was blowing sparks from it. "You're coming to Wearmouth?" I asked.

"No," he said. "*You* are coming to Plymouth."

"But I don't want to go to Plymouth!" I said.

He shrugged. "Then you are free to leave the ship now," he said.

"How do I get to shore?" I asked.

"'*And lo, when Peter was come down out of the ship, he walked on the water*'," Drake said. He laughed suddenly and looked at me. "Listen, Marsden. Her Majesty needs this ship for her secret Pacific venture. And this ship needs a navigator. You are the only navigator Captain Milburn has got. Would you betray Her Majesty and desert her now?"

"Why, no."

"Then you will sail with us to South America. You'll come home rich," he said, jabbing the stem of his pipe at me.

"I'd rather go home now," I groaned. "My father will wonder what's happened to me."

"You can send a message from Plymouth. I'm joining my flagship, *Pelican*, there along with the *Elizabeth*, the

Marigold and the *Christopher*. We sail on the fifteenth of November and you'll be with us."

"Yes, sir," I said. I felt a strange dizziness.

"Of course, you could always go ashore at Plymouth and desert us, couldn't you?" he said. He stepped down to where I stood on the main deck. He threw a strong arm around my shoulders and clutched me till it hurt. "But then I would have to track you down and kill you, James Marsden." He took the bowl of his pipe in his hand and pulled the mouthpiece across my throat. "No one must be left ashore to betray us to Spanish spies. It would hurt me deeply to have to kill you. And you wouldn't want to hurt me, would you?"

"No, sir."

"Then cheer up, James. You're off on the greatest adventure of your life!"

It was almost dark in the garden when my father finished his tale. There was a soft chuckling from Grandfather. "I sent you off to see the world," he said. "I didn't think you'd be seeing quite so much of it!"

Great-Uncle George joined in the laughter and I was glad that the shadows hid my own smile.

"I was lucky to be part of history," said my father.

"Or unlucky enough to be kidnapped," Grandmother snapped.

"I wasn't kidnapped!" said Father. "I was proud to serve my queen."

"Even if you had to be kidnapped to do it," Great-Uncle George teased.

I thought my father's temper would rise, but we were interrupted by the steward walking down the path to the main gates set in the wall, as he did every evening at sunset. He carried a lantern in his left hand and swung the gate shut with his right. As he was about to slide the bar across, the gate was suddenly pushed open. The steward staggered back and held up the lantern. It lit a ragged little man with a round yellow face and deep, dark pools of shadow round his eyes. He held a seaman's cap in his stained hands. He peered at the family where we sat in the garden.

"Sir James?" he said uncertainly.

"Captain Walsh?" my father cried, jumping to his feet. "Why aren't you with our ship, the *Pelican II*? She should be off the coast of Yorkshire by now."

"Oh, Sir James, sir," said the man, "she's off the coast of Durham on some rocks. She's wrecked, Sir James, sir. Wrecked."

CHAPTER FOUR

"I shall never see my gold again"

My father gave a cry of despair. "My money! All my money in that ship."

But my mother stood up and walked over to the man. "Are you all right, Captain Walsh?" she asked.

"Yes, madam."

"And your crew?"

"All saved. A few scrapes and bruises and a bit of a soaking, but they're all alive."

"That's something to be thankful for," my mother told him.

My father jumped to his feet. "Thankful! Thankful? We could be ruined, Marion, and you say we should be *thankful*."

"Twenty men are alive and their families will be thankful," she said gently.

My father would not be calmed. "But not for long. I'll take them to court. They are common criminals. They have tried to ruin me and I *shall* ruin them." He marched across to the miserable seaman and shouted into his face. "The *Pelican II* was unsinkable. What happened?"

"There was a sudden squall from the east and we were driven towards the coast. Before the crew could lower the sails we were being driven on to Blackhall Rocks."

"Why were you so close to the shore, you fool?"

"Because we'd have got lost if we went out of sight of land, Sir James."

"You couldn't get lost. You had charts, didn't you?"

"And a navigator?" my grandfather put in.

"No," the poor man answered.

"No? Why not?"

"Sir James refused to pay for one. I asked who would navigate and he said a blind man could find his way from Wearmouth to London. Those were his very words. He said he wanted to save money."

My father's lips were moving, but no words were coming out. Suddenly he turned on his heel and marched into Marsden Hall.

My mother turned to Meg. "Would you take Captain Walsh into the kitchen, please? See that he has food and drink. It was good of him to come all this way to give us the news. Any other man would have been unable to travel for a week after a shock like that. You are a gallant man, Captain Walsh."

"Thank you, madam," the man muttered as Meg led him away.

The family walked slowly into the main hall of our home. The steward had made up a small fire in the great hearth and lit candles around the room. The tapestries hanging from the walls looked as dull and gloomy as the faces of the people who gathered there.

"It's a loss," Grandfather said. "James may have been too ambitious. People who reach for the stars often stumble over molehills."

"Will we be poor?" I asked.

Grandfather and Great-Uncle George looked at one another. There was some movement of eyebrows as they exchanged silent thoughts. "Not exactly," Grandfather said finally. "But all our fortunes rest on the second ship, the Hawk," he explained.

Grandfather had managed the Marsden estate wisely for more years than most men live. But even he wasn't prepared for someone like Miles Glub.

We had our first visit from Master Glub just three days after the disaster with the *Pelican II*. They had been a miserable three days for me. I had been forced to sit in the library with my father, poring over sheets of figures, adding and subtracting and moving money from column to column. Whichever way we looked at it there was not enough to pay the first part of the loan when it was due.

Then, on the fourth morning after news of the wreck of the *Pelican II*, the steward tapped on the door and announced, "There's a Master Glub to see you, Sir James. He is waiting in the gallery."

My father rubbed his weary eyes with his hands and sighed. "He's come to talk about his money," he said with a voice like doom. "Come, William. Let us face this together."

The man in the gallery was huge. He stood with his fat legs planted wide apart and his fists on his hips. I had seen a portrait of King Henry VIII where he posed like that. But this man was not dressed like the King. He had a shirt of fine white linen, but it was grubby around the cuffs and collar and the seams were split by his bulky body. He wore a light, sleeveless jerkin of rich blue velvet over the shirt, but it was spoiled with stains and crusted food down the front. He wasn't wearing a hat and his shining, sweating head was completely hairless, like some monstrous egg.

He was looking at the portraits of the Marsden family that hung on the walls of the gallery, and turned towards us as we entered. He had a pink shaved face and a curious twisted smile. "Sir James!" he said. His voice was ridiculously light for so huge a man.

"Master Glub," my father said. He was about to say something else, but Glub lumbered round to face me.

"This must be your young lad that you're so proud of. You must be Walter?"

"William, sir," I said.

"William! That's right! I remember now! I am Miles Glub." He held out a soft and sticky hand. I shook it and tried to stop myself wiping my hand on my doublet.

"I'm pleased to see you, sir," I said.

"I like you, young Will!" he said suddenly. "Whatever happens to Marsden Hall, I'll see that you are provided for."

I had no idea what he was talking about. "Sir?"

"I heard about your disaster with the *Polecat*," he said.

"The *Pelican II*," my father said. "Named after Francis Drake's flagship."

"Polecat – pelican – I knew it was some kind of animal. Anyway, I was very sad to hear about your loss." The man's eyes were as shiny as the beads of sweat that ran down his face. He didn't look too sorry.

My father forced a smile. "I am glad that you have called, Miles," he said. "I am sure you will extend the date for the loan."

"Oh no, James," said Miles Glub, trying to look disappointed. "We have an agreement. And a man's word is his bond." He turned back to look at the family portraits that stared down at him from the gallery wall. "I think I will take these paintings when I take over Marsden Hall," he said.

"What does he mean?" I asked my father.

"I mean that *I* will be the new owner of Marsden Hall," Glub said. He showed his mottled teeth in a satisfied grin. "I lent the Marsden family three thousand pounds. If I am not repaid on time, I take Marsden Hall."

"The family's lived here for hundreds of years," I said.

"Yes. Sad, isn't it? I'm sure you'll find somewhere smaller. A cottage in Low Street could be yours for fifty pounds."

"We couldn't live in a place like Low Street!" I said.

Suddenly he poked his head forward so that folds of chin rolled over his dirty collar. "Why not, boy? I did! I was born in a place like Low Street. A filthy, rat-infested hole of a place. And I had to go and work in a Tyneside pit cutting coal for rich men like your father. But I saved my money, young William. I saved and bought a cart to carry the coals. And I bought more carts and I laid wooden rails to make wagon ways and I moved more coal on the Tyne than anyone else. And I made my fortune. So what's wrong with living in a place like Low Street?" he asked.

"Nothing, sir," I mumbled.

"Nothing, sir," he mimicked in his squeaking voice. "Nothing wrong with the *Glubs* living there, but it's not good enough for the mighty Marsdens, is that what you are saying?"

"No, sir."

"No, sir. Well, now I have enough money to buy a place like Marsden Hall – and I've always wanted to live in a house like this. At least I *had* enough money, but I lent it to your father, didn't I? I lent it so he could build the unsinkable *Polecat* and now it's *wrecked*. And so, young William, are the Marsden family! Ha! Your first payment is due at noon in ten days' time, Sir James. You have ten days and not one day more to pay me one thousand pounds. One thousand pounds a month for the next three months. One minute late, with one payment, and Marsden Hall is mine."

"I know the terms of the agreement," my father said miserably. "You'll have your money."

"I doubt it, Sir James," the man said with a shake of his shining globe of a head. "I doubt it."

He looked lovingly at the dark portraits. The ancient, long-dead faces seemed to frown back at him. Then he walked out of the gallery without a backward glance.

My father stared through the windows into the garden for a long time. The door into the passageway opened slowly and Meg looked in. "What a terrible man!" she said.

"He wants to take Marsden Hall from us," I said.

"I know, I overheard," she said, then blushed quickly. "Accidentally overheard. But you won't let him, will you?"

"I'm not sure I can stop him," I said.

My father turned his head slowly and looked at us with dull, lifeless eyes. He was a defeated man. I only wish he could have cared about his family the way he cared about the house. I couldn't feel sorry for him, or offer him any comfort. It was left for Meg to approach him.

"The *Hawk* is nearly finished, isn't it?" she asked. "Couldn't you take a load of coal to London and sell it?"

"The *Hawk* is finished," he said. "But she would have to make two trips to London to make a thousand pounds. One load is ready, but two would be impossible in the time we have left."

"What about the fortune you set off to find with Captain Drake?" she asked. "Don't you have any of that left?"

He turned back to the window and didn't answer for a

long time. "Drake's treasure," he whispered. "Drake's treasure. He promised me the money . . . but he died six years ago before I was paid. A gentleman doesn't like to pester another gentleman for a debt."

"So where is it?"

"His second wife, Lady Drake, will be holding the money."

"We could ask her for it, and pay off Master Glub!" Meg cried.

My father shook his head. "We'd have to go to Plymouth. No one could ride to Plymouth and back in ten days."

"But we could sail," I said.

He closed his eyes and thought for a while. "We can load the *Hawk* with coal tonight and set sail tomorrow morning. Sell the coal in London and sail on to Plymouth. With a good navigator – and fair winds – we could just make it."

"Have we time to find a navigator?" I asked.

My father's helpless expression began to harden. "You are forgetting, boy. Captain Geordie Milburn himself called me the finest navigator ever to set foot on the deck of a ship. I am the only man in England who could make that trip in time. I know every tide and current and sandbank and headland from here to Plymouth."

"You'll need a good captain," I said.

"I will captain my own ship," he told me. "I can do it, you know. Sailors respect me. I know the sea and I know ships."

He'd recovered quickly from his gloomy mood and was as arrogant as ever. "I wish I could come with you," I said.

"Come with me? Of course you will have to come with me," he said. "I will teach you everything you need to know about sailing. One day you can captain a collier yourself."

In my dreams I didn't see myself captaining a collier. I saw myself acting on a stage in London. But at least if I went along I would be able to get to London and make my own way when I got there. This was the chance I'd been waiting for.

My father's excitement was starting to infect me and Meg caught it too. "And me, Sir James. You have to take *me* with you."

"A woman on a ship is bad luck. It makes the sea angry."

"I'm not a woman, I'm a girl," said Meg. "And I'll make a great ship's cook."

"We don't have a cook," my father admitted.

"Let her come with us," I said. I knew it was dangerous to try to stop Meg from doing something when she was determined.

My father was hurrying down the gallery towards the pantry where he found the steward and started giving orders for packing our bags. "Not *black* bags, mark you! Black bags bring bad luck to a whole ship."

He called the ostler and ordered him to saddle a fast horse and act as a messenger to the shipyards. "Take this to the foreman of the rigging crew," my father said, writing furiously and sealing a letter with a mess of wax before the ink had dried. "I know he can read. And take this one to the chandler at Southwick. Have the ship supplied with food and the water casks filled."

I looked on helplessly and tried to see where I could be of use. Everyone else in the house seemed to be working to make our rescue of Marsden Hall a success. And no one wanted me under their feet. Mother and Grandmother arranged for spare cooking equipment to be taken from our kitchen to the Hawk.

Grandfather and Great-Uncle George made urgent plans to rescue the charts and navigation equipment from the *Pelican II*. Captain Walsh said she was resting on Blackhall Rocks and slowly breaking up with each tide. He'd left a man on board to guard it from wreckers. Grandfather arranged for everything useful to go straight to Southwick and the new ship. "Anchors, sails, rope and tackle – even the cabin lanterns and hammocks. Everything!"

The whole house was in an uproar, but no one was panicking. "But what can *I* do?" I asked my mother.

She stopped and looked at me thoughtfully. "Your turn'll come, Will. If you want to do something useful, you could go to the church and say some prayers."

I walked through the village to the church and slipped into the cool, dim building that was older than Marsden Hall itself. I knelt and closed my eyes and tried to imagine a life without these familiar places. God didn't seem to be home that day. Perhaps because I was praying for myself.

I decided to walk through Bournmoor Woods and down to the river. The path wound past Widow Atkinson's cottage and on to the bridge over the River Wear. Meg had once dragged me out of the river at this spot and probably saved my life. Sadness swept over me the way water had washed over my head that night when I'd almost drowned.

I trudged back up the path. Widow Atkinson was in her garden, tending herbs and watering some of them. "What's wrong, Master Will?" she asked.

I needed someone to talk to. Everyone at the hall was too busy. I told her the story. She was very old, but her eyes were as bright as a child's. She listened silently until I had finished. "So, you're sad because you may never see Marsden Hall again?"

"Of course," I said.

"Happiness is in your head, not in a pile of stones," she said. "That Miles Glub could be right, Will Marsden. Some people have to live in places like Low Street and places like my poor cottage."

"Marsden Hall's my home."

"And you're saying goodbye to Marsden, aren't you?"

"No," I muttered.

"You say you're fond of the place. Then why do you want to leave it? You want to go to London and be an actor, don't you?"

"Yes, but I want to come home some day," I said.

"You want a lot, young man. If you want something, you have to work for it. You are planning to run away and let your family look after the Hall so you'll have somewhere to come home to? Is that it?"

"Yes . . . no!" I stammered. I was confused. I wanted sympathy and was only getting hard truths.

"I'll tell you why you're so miserable, Will Marsden," she said, waving a long, thin finger under my nose. "You're miserable because you're planning to betray your family. When the ship reaches London, you mean to leave the ship and desert your father when he needs you."

"No!" I said fiercely.

"You wouldn't be so upset if it weren't true," she said simply.

And she was right. I was worried. If an old wise woman could see into my heart, then who else could?

CHAPTER FIVE

"I desire no more delight than to be under sail and gone tonight"

"Saints preserve us!" my father cried.

The morning after Glub's visit, we were riding to the port where the *Hawk* lay when my father reined in his horse.

"What's wrong?" Meg asked.

"There's a man on the path with red hair. And he's walking towards us."

"So?"

"So it is terribly bad luck to meet a red-haired man when you're on your way to join a ship," he hissed.

"It's too late now to avoid him," I sighed.

"No! No! No! You can defeat the curse if you speak to him before he speaks to you. Stay here." Father spurred his horse forward. While he was still fifty paces away from the man, he cried, "Good day to you, sir! It's a fine day, isn't it?"

The man pulled down the corners of his mouth and plodded on past my father. When he reached Meg and me, he muttered, "It's a terrible life being red-haired when you live near a port." Meg grinned as he went on. "For the sake of sweet Jesus, don't tell him I have flat feet too."

We rode on to join my father. "What if he'd had flat feet?" I asked.

"Disaster," my father cried, "utter disaster!"

"Anything else?" Meg asked.

"Lots of things I learned from Drake," my father said. "When you step on to the gangplank you must never put your left foot down first, or you are doomed."

"Which foot should I put down?" Meg asked innocently.

"Your *right* foot," he replied, failing to see the joke.

"Flowers on a ship mean a funeral – oh, and don't look back as we leave the port, or you may never return. Don't use the word 'drown' when we're at sea, or cut your nails or hair."

"No, Sir James," Meg said seriously. "Sailors seem to be very superstitious."

"But not as superstitious as actors," I murmured. I'd spoken to many of them when they brought a touring show to the marketplace in Durham and had made a journey to the Borders of Scotland with an actor named Hugh Richmond. While my father was busy planning the voyage, I'd been finding Hugh's address in London.

When we rounded the last bend in the river we could see the *Hawk* below us. The crew, directed by Captain Walsh, were still preparing rigging and storing equipment. But my eye was caught by the figure that sat on a bay horse at the end of the gangplank, watching the preparations. "What sort of luck is it if you meet a fat bald man on your way to the ship?" I asked.

My father squinted down to the quay where the man sat. "Miles Glub," he snarled. "What does he want?"

I was sure we'd find out very soon and rode on to meet him. The man was smiling as we approached.

"What are you doing here?" my father asked coldly.

"Checking that my money is safe," Glub said.

"We will have your money within the ten days."

"Really? How will you do that?"

"That's none of your business, Glub."

"Oh, but it *is*, Sir James. For all I know you could be running away from Durham. I may never see you again."

"Would I desert my wife, my parents and my home?" Father demanded.

"You might, Sir James. You're the man I made the agreement with. It is *you* that I must take before a court in Durham to get my hands on Marsden Hall."

"Not if I pay you."

"But you *can't* and you *won't*, Sir James. I want to know where you are going."

"And I am not prepared to tell you."

"Then I will come with you," the coal dealer said.

"You can't do that!"

"Of course I can. I will stable my horse here on the quayside and make some arrangements. Then I'll join you in an hour's time. Captain Walsh tells me you sail with the tide."

"There is no room in any of the cabins," my father told him.

"Sir James! Sir James! You forget I have spent most of my life sleeping on floors because we couldn't afford a bed. It's summer and I shall be quite happy to sleep on the deck of your ship. I will see you in an hour," he said, and walked his horse past the quayside warehouses towards the taverns.

Meg took our horses and followed him while Father and I took the saddle packs and began to stow them on the ship. "Right foot first!" he warned me as we climbed the gangplank.

The ship smelled of new wood and tar. The decks were

already stained with a trail of black marks where the coal had been loaded into the hold. My father called across to the sailor who had been captain of *Pelican II*. "This will have to be washed down once we're at sea, Walsh."

"Yes, sir. I'll tell the crew."

"No. *I* will tell the crew. I will act as captain on this trip. You will be my first lieutenant."

"Anything you say, Sir James. The men are just grateful that you're giving them another chance after . . . after their little accident on your other ship."

My father snorted down his thin nose. "Accident! Ha! Stupidity and clumsiness. I did not employ these men because they are good sailors, Walsh. I employed them because they survived. They are clearly lucky sailors. As Francis Drake always said, 'Surround yourself with lucky sailors and you can't go wrong.'"

He strutted around the deck and checked every detail of the ship. He looked at the mast and decided against climbing it. "William! Climb to the top of the mast."

"What?"

"Don't stand there with your mouth open catching flies. Climb to the top of the mast."

"How?"

"Climb the ratlines." I looked at him blankly. "The rope ladders on the mast."

I struggled upwards, my feet becoming tangled with the rope "rungs" and my hands burning as I gripped the rope supports too tightly. If I looked down at my feet, I could see a frightening drop to the deck. If I looked up at my hands, my feet failed to find the rungs. The crew stopped their work to watch me battle towards a wooden platform. I finally pulled myself on to it. There was a light breeze up there and the view was fine. I could see clear over the forest of masts to the North Sea and back up the Wear Valley to the Pennine Hills.

My father was shouting something. "What?" I asked, cupping a hand to my ear.

"Crow's-nest. The very top!"

I looked up. There was another platform still higher. He wanted me to go up there! I took a deep breath and tried to climb with my eyes closed. Somehow I made it. This topmost platform was swinging in the wind like a willow tree in a gale. I was sure it would whip me out like a catapult.

"What can you see?" my father cried up to me.

"I can see *you*."

"I meant on the *river*, you foolish boy! Any movement?"

"Yes, the river's moving."

"I mean any *ships* leaving the quay. Are other ships preparing to leave?"

I peered downriver and saw ships moving. Some were being towed by crews in rowing boats while others were letting the tide carry them out. "Yes!" I called back.

My father called an order to the crew and they moved to the front of the ship. I knew I'd have to learn to call that the "bow", but at that moment I was wondering what they were doing. They began to haul on a thick rope and minutes later the anchor was pulled up. We were setting sail!

I looked across to the taverns and saw Meg sprinting over the cobbled quayside and on to the wooden pier where we were tied up. She leapt on to the gangplank and almost collided with a sailor who was walking down it. They snatched at one another in a mad dance and swayed in each other's arms. For a moment it looked as if they were both going to fall in the river, but they recovered and Meg tumbled on to the deck.

The sailor ran down the gangplank and began to unfasten the rope that tied us to the pier. There was a high-pitched cry and I looked down to see Miles Glub hurrying from the tavern with a leather bag in his fat paw. He was calling, "Stop!" while my father on the deck urged the man to hurry with the rope.

The rope at the back – sorry, the "stern" – was unfastened, but before the man could reach the bow rope he was in the clutch of Glub's mighty hand. The sailor crumpled like an eggshell under his grip. Glub threw him to the ground and started to unwind the rope from its post on the pier. He held it in his hand and laughed. "Going somewhere, Sir James?" he called. The ship was being tugged by the tide, but Glub held it easily.

Suddenly he flung the rope on to the deck and moved quickly to the gangplank. He ran up it and it bounced dangerously before he landed on the deck. The unlucky sailor scrambled after him and hauled the plank up before it dropped into the water. My father was too busy at the tiller to deal with Glub at that moment. The *Hawk* drifted mid-stream and down towards the sea. A pilot in a large oared vessel threw a line on to the ship and guided us past the other vessels in the river.

I forgot my father's warning. I turned and looked back. I could see the fields, yellow-gold and green stripes of corn and grass. There was a dark patch that I knew was Bournmoor Woods and a tiny speck of grey that was Marsden Hall. I watched it till we were out of the river mouth and wondered when I'd see it again.

The pilot cast off our line and the crew lowered a sail. The wind caught it and the sail opened with a crack, bending the mast so sharply that I was flung forward. I'd have crashed to the deck if I hadn't snatched at a rope.

"That'll teach you to keep your wits about you!" my father called from his place at the stern. "Come down now and I'll send a proper lookout up to guide us."

Getting down was worse than climbing up. I groped for every foothold and was sure each one would give way if I lowered my weight on to it. I staggered on to the safety of the deck and found Meg's sea-green eyes looking at me with amusement. She'd changed into a shirt and hose. Her hair was tied back in a black ribbon and she could have passed for a cabin boy. "Shall we see your acrobatic display every day, Will?" she asked, laughing. "It was better than the tumblers at Chester-le-Street market!"

I was about to make an angry reply when my father called, "All hands on deck."

The sailors finished their tasks and assembled on the main deck while my father looked down on them from the raised stern deck. "I have some good news for you men," he said over the noises of the ship and the sea. "I shall not be punishing you for wrecking the *Pelican II*. However, I shall not be paying you for this trip."

The men looked sullen and rebellious. They knew the punishment for mutiny was hanging, but crews that stood together against their captain could get away with it. Of course the captain would have to disappear over the side of the ship in an "accident" so he couldn't give evidence against them. They were looking at me and I realized that I would have to be killed along with my father. It may have been the strange ox of a man, Miles Glub, that held them back. They didn't know whose side he was on and they didn't think they could lift him off the deck, let alone over the side!

"It was Captain Walsh's fault!" a deck hand cried. "What if he sinks us this time? We'll be risking our lives for nothing!"

There was a cheer of agreement. My father raised a hand. "*I* will be your captain on this trip."

There was uneasy laughter from the men. Someone said loudly, "Then we're doomed, lads!"

My father glared at the man and said, "I am the finest sailor in the north!"

"What? You?" There was more laughter.

Then he said a few words that silenced them. "I sailed with Drake."

Sea spray hissed against the bows and the sails slapped in the breeze. A seagull screamed overhead, but there was no sound from the men on the deck. My father puffed out his chest. "How many Englishmen have sailed the Pacific Ocean, eh? Not many. Why, I'd guess most of you have never even sailed the Atlantic. But you are looking at a man who has sailed around the world and lived to tell the tale. Queen Elizabeth herself chose me because she had heard of my skill as a navigator."

The crew no longer looked mutinous. They looked just what they were. Simple family men who worked as hard as they had to in order to make a living, but worked less hard if they had the chance. And this was the chance.

"Tell us about Drake," the deck hand shouted.

Father took a deep breath and tilted back his head. "Captain Walsh – I mean, Lieutenant Walsh!"

"Yes, sir?" the former captain answered.

"Take the tiller and keep the compass on south by south-west."

"Yes, sir."

The men sank down on to the deck, glad of the rest, while Father sat on the stairs that led down from the stern deck. Miles Glub fastened a large red handkerchief around his head to keep the warm afternoon sun from burning his bald pate and sat on a hatch cover. Every eye was turned towards Father. Only Meg, cooking in the ship's galley, and the young sailor in the crow's-nest were unable to listen to his tale . . .

SIR JAMES MARSDEN'S STORY

Francis Drake's trip to the Pacific was a secret, my friends. It was so great a secret that even the sailors didn't know about it! They thought they were off on a trip to the Mediterranean. Drake didn't tell them they were going to South America.

Of course there was always the chance that the men would mutiny when they found out, so Drake took along a few gentlemen like myself who were in on the great secret. If the crew turned nasty, some sharp swordplay from trained fighters like me would soon bring a little order.

As it happened it was the *gentlemen* who caused a lot of the trouble. But Drake couldn't have known that when we set off from Plymouth that November evening. He led the way in the *Pelican*, then there was the *Elizabeth*, while I followed in Captain Geordie Milburn's ship, the *Swan*. It was no larger than this ship, a simple North Sea trader. The last two ships, the *Marigold* and the *Christopher*, were even smaller.

Five ships, a hundred and sixty-four crew – some of them boys even younger than my own son is now. People ask me what Drake was like. I can tell you, he was a great man.

We'd been at sea a week before I noticed that Drake never appeared after eight at night. "He says his prayers in his cabin," said Simon Wood, Drake's navigator, when he came across to the *Swan* one day.

"I know he's a very religious man," I said.

"Of course there are some men who say he prays to the Devil," said William Barrett.

"That's the sort of nonsense the Spanish spout," said Wood. "They say he has a spirit with him in his cabin. Well, I've never seen it."

Hawkins lowered his voice. "I've seen it. And I've heard it!"

I was shocked at the idea I was sailing with a servant of the Devil. "A spirit? Is it a cat?"

Barrett looked pleased with himself. "It's a drum. You hear it beating when Drake goes into his cabin to pray."

"That's just him tapping it. Why, I've seen you tap the table when you're doing some hard bit of arithmetic!" Wood said.

William Barrett looked over his shoulder as if the Devil himself was lurking near. "So, how come I've heard that drum beating when Drake was *out* of his cabin?"

Sailors are a superstitious lot, as you know. But that was one story I didn't want to believe. "He knows the Bible like a priest!" I said.

"Aha!" said Barrett. "And, if I were a devil, I'd make a point of learning the Bible." He wagged a finger at Wood and me. "Drake has more lives than a witch's cat. You'll see, you'll see."

Drake could be ruthless, cruel and wild at times. I was upset by the stories of the devil drum. But by the time we'd crossed the Atlantic to South America, something had happened to take my mind off Drake's witchcraft.

The true seamen loved Drake – they cursed him when they found they were really headed for South America, but they forgave him.

The gentlemen were harder to tame. Those gentlemen were not so popular with Drake's sailors. They refused to dirty their hands by pulling ropes and heaving sails. They treated the sailors like servants, and Drake didn't like that. But none of us knew how much he really hated some of those gentlemen.

Then, one wintry afternoon, Drake signalled to us on the *Swan* that he wanted to come aboard. He drew the *Pelican* alongside and we saw that he had a gentleman called Thomas Doughty lashed to the mast with ropes. Drake called across, "Geordie Milburn! I've had as much of this man as my stomach can bear. I want him out of my sight. I want you to take him."

Geordie looked grim and muttered to me, "Drake's temper will be the death of someone, James, you'll see."

I watched, amazed, as Thomas Doughty was untied from the mast and started to struggle with the men holding him. "I am commander of the soldiers when we reach shore!" he was crying. "You've got no right to do this, Drake."

"We're not on shore now, Doughty. I am in command when we're at sea, and you'll do as I tell you. Get off my ship and on to the *Swan*."

"I refuse."

"Then I'll fasten you to a rope, hoist you on to a spar and swing you across like a sack of ship's biscuits."

Doughty kept struggling for a few minutes, but, in the end, gave in and allowed himself to be lowered into a boat and rowed across to us.

My friend, Captain Geordie Milburn, was one of the finest men you could wish to meet. He had no hatred in his heart for anyone and he welcomed Doughty aboard. "What an honour, Master Doughty. What have you done to upset our friend Drake?"

Doughty was a red-faced man with a thick brown beard and eyebrows that met above his nose. He seemed to have a scowl set permanently on his face.

"You were there when we sailed by Cape Blanco and captured that rich Portuguese ship, weren't you?"

"A fine prize," Geordie said. "My navigator James Marsden and I have spent many hours talking about how we'll spend our share of the treasure."

"What treasure?" Doughty snarled. "Have you *seen* any treasure?"

"No," I told him. "It's on board the *Pelican* with Drake."

"So, why isn't he letting you *see* what's there?" Doughty asked and didn't wait for an answer. "I'll tell you why. Because he plans to cheat you when we get back to England. He'll tell you that there are two chests of gold to share when there are fifty. He'll keep the rest for himself."

"Drake is an honest man," said Geordie.

"You stupid little northern coal-bucket owner!" Doughty raged. "Drake is a lowborn little seaman, just like you, Milburn. He has no idea how to command men. When he needs soldiers to fight the Spaniards, it is the *gentlemen* who will be training them. Without men like me to help, Drake is nothing."

Geordie waited till Doughty's storm had blown itself out. "I'll have some fresh straw put down in the hold for you, Master Doughty," he said mildly.

Doughty's eyes began to bulge. He lunged forward and grabbed Geordie by the jerkin. "The hold! Slaves sleep in a hold. I want a cabin. I demand a cabin!"

My captain bent back the fingers that clutched his clothing. "The people who do the most work get the best quarters. You are an adventurer, Master Doughty."

"That's right. I've put money into this voyage, so I expect better treatment."

"James Marsden has put money into it too, haven't you, James?"

"A hundred pounds," I told Doughty.

"But James here is working as a navigator too," Geordie explained. "And James hasn't upset Captain Drake. What did you do, Master Doughty?"

"I was trying to explain. Drake told us that no one must touch the Portuguese treasure chests, or speak to the Portuguese prisoners."

"You disobeyed?"

"I went with Drake's own brother, Tom, just to have a look. To make sure that we weren't cheated. It so happened that the prisoners gave me a pair of gloves, some money and a ring. But I did not steal them, as Drake says."

"You *did* disobey a captain's order. And the captain's word is law at sea the way the Queen's word is law in England," I pointed out. I'd studied law books in my lessons back at Marsden and was very clear about duty.

"Shut up, you pompous little northern starveling," Doughty said to me. "You are so full of wind that if I stuck my knife in you, you'd burst with enough air to fill a hundred sails."

Geordie drew himself up to his full height. "That is no way to speak to my navigator, Master Doughty. James works hard at his job even though he is an investor, like you. That's why James will eat with the crew the same as I do. You will eat what you are given."

"I would not want to eat with the crew like some common seaman," Doughty sneered. "You are no more a gentleman than Drake is."

"True," Geordie agreed. "Still, it's better to be a well-fed common seaman than a starving gentleman."

"I'm not starving," Doughty said.

Geordie gave one of his huge smiles. "Oh, but you will be after a day or so of living on the scraps from my crew's table. Now get below decks and find yourself a corner in the hold. Keep out of my way, or you will be drinking sea water and eating your bed straw."

Doughty was breathing hard. He pushed his face close to my captain's. "When we get back to England, I will see you hang, Milburn."

"I've heard you get a good view from on top of the gallows tree," was the reply.

Doughty turned his glare on me. "And you will be swinging by his side," he promised.

"If I'm as full of wind as you say, I'll probably blow away," I told him. I was pleased with that reply. Doughty raised a hand to strike me, but Geordie stopped him and dragged him off to the hold.

We ate well on the *Swan* as we crossed the Atlantic. We passed through shoals of fish with wings that flew over the deck where we could catch them.

We reached the coast of America in April. Birds were landing on the deck, so tame we could walk up and club them. And all the while Doughty had to survive on mouldering biscuits and salted herrings. Geordie Milburn made him pay for his insults.

Of course Captain Drake was going to make him pay even more dearly.

CHAPTER SIX

"There be land rats
and water rats
– I mean pirates"

The crew were sitting listening spellbound to my father's story, and I was beginning to understand how he'd become such a harsh magistrate back at Marsden Manor. Father had a simple idea of right and wrong that he'd learned when he sailed with Drake: obey, or be punished.

I suspected that he was making his own part in the story more important than it really was. Perhaps his memory really let him believe he had stood shoulder to shoulder with Captain Milburn and faced the furious Thomas Doughty. Or perhaps he'd been braver when he was a young man.

Still, I was as interested in his story as the gaping, wide-eyed crew. I'd have wanted to listen all afternoon if we hadn't been interrupted by the lookout. "Ship off the port bow!" he cried. There was something in the tone of his voice that made everyone jump. There had been lots of ships passing us since we'd left the River Wear. Most of them were small fishing vessels from the Durham coast, a few were traders on their way home from London. This one was different.

The timbers of the ship were so dark they were almost

black. The sails were yellow with age and patched more times than a beggar's cloak. The black ship was ploughing along a course that would meet ours in about a mile. Unless she was heading for the cliffs, it was hard to see why her captain would want to take that course.

"She's flying the red flag," my father said briskly. "That means she's a pirate."

Miles Glub struggled to his feet. "Don't be ridiculous, Sir James. What would a band of pirates want with a load of coal?"

My father was running up the steps to the tiller. He pushed ex-captain Walsh roughly out of the way and began rapidly giving orders and answering questions. "Full sail!" he shouted to the crew, who scurried to obey. "They aren't after the coal, Glub, they're after our ship. It's a new ship and theirs must be rotten."

"There's not room for anyone else on this ship," said Glub.

"I know. That's why they'll put us on board their ship . . . if we're lucky."

A deck hand gave me a rope and told me to start pulling if I wanted to save my life. It was attached to a heavy spar and I struggled with the stiff new pulleys. "Help me, Master Glub!" I called.

He wandered across the deck and took a grip on the rope. "What does he mean, 'If we're lucky'?" he asked.

"He means they'll throw us in the sea and let us swim for shore if we're *un*lucky," I explained.

"I can't swim!" he cried.

"Then you'll be one of the unlucky ones," I told him. "You'd better start pulling."

He heaved on the rope and it came free suddenly. The sail rattled up the mast and caught the wind. The ship surged forward. "But what's he trying to do?" Glub asked.

"I guess we're trying to outrun the pirates."

"You can't outrun pirates. Not with a fully loaded collier."

"Trust him," I said. I climbed up to where my father stood holding the tiller. "What can I do?" I asked.

"Hold this tiller, boy, while I chart us a course."

I grabbed the heavy beam and held it exactly where my father indicated as he bent over his charts. "Where are we?" he asked.

Meg chose that moment to appear on the stern deck, a large wet fish dripping in her hand. "What's happening?"

"Pirates," I said, nodding towards the black ship. It was close enough now to see figures on the decks. Their clothes were drab, but something bright was glinting in their hands.

"What can *I* fight with?" Meg asked, her eyes sparkling at the thought.

"We're not armed, girl," Father snapped. "We'll just have to outsail them."

Glub lumbered up the stairs to join us. It was becoming crowded. He scanned the sea to the north. "Are there no other ships to come to our rescue? A collier can't outrun a frigate," he said again.

My father scoured the map and answered without raising his hand. "I said outsail, not outrun."

"What's the difference?"

"If I knew where we were, I'd have time to explain. But I don't, so kindly be quiet, Master Glub."

Meg jumped up on the rail around the deck and looked to the west. "I know where we are!" she cried.

"What do you mean?"

"There! Look! It's the wreck of the *Pelican II*! We must be just off Blackhall Rocks!"

"Perfect!" my father cried. He threw some charts aside and

found a sheet that showed the Durham coast. "Lieutenant Walsh!" he shouted. "As much sail as we can. Go down on deck and organize the men while I steer to shore."

"You're going to run us aground?" Glub cried. "That's good, I can't swim, you know. I'll feel safer if we're on the shore."

"And if we run aground, you'll have no chance of getting your money."

"But much, much more chance of getting my hands on your house! Carry on, Captain Marsden." He walked off the stern deck cackling like the seagulls overhead.

The captain of the black ship had seen our change of direction and swung round to track us. "Can we really hope to outsail her, Sir James?" Meg asked.

"We have a new ship," he said. "The longer a ship is at sea the more it gets encrusted with weed and shellfish. They drag on the hull and slow it down. Now, Francis Drake drew his ships on to sandy beaches every few months and scraped the bottom of his fleet clean. From the look of that pirate, I don't think he'd bother. There comes a time when the hull is scraped so thin it leaks like an old bucket. His ship is probably like that. That'll be why he wants the *Hawk*."

"But we're fully loaded with coal," I said.

"And he's probably full of water," Father said calmly. "It makes it a fair race."

I'd never known my father was a sportsman, interested in a race. Especially when we could die if we lost.

He turned back to the chart and then looked towards the sorry wreckage of our first ship. We were hurrying towards the splintered timbers and the foaming waters around it. "Take us to port!" he ordered me.

"Which port?" I asked stupidly.

"He means turn us left!" Meg cried, waving and splashing me with the stinking water from the fish in her hand.

"Why didn't he say so?" I grumbled.

"Because he's a proper sailor. He says port for left and starboard for right."

She pointed the way I should turn the rudder. Sometimes her cleverness irritated me like a fleabite.

The ship swayed and Father gave orders for changes of sail. Our sudden turn had put the black ship in line behind us. If I looked over my shoulder, I could see the grinning faces of unshaven men getting closer every minute.

There was a flash of light from the muzzle of a cannon. Moments later I heard the boom of the explosion and the crack as the cannonball hit a spar and cracked it. "They're trying to sink us!" I cried.

Father kept his head moving from the chart to the shore ahead, following our course on the map with his finger. He ignored the black ship. "They want this ship with as little damage as possible," he said. "That was just a warning. They're trying to stop us from running aground."

"It would spoil their plans," I said. "Is that what you're planning to do to us?"

"That's what I want them to *think* I'm doing," my father replied. "Of course a sensible captain would run his ship on to a beach so his crew got off safely. They could put a line on the *Hawk* and pull her off with very little trouble."

"But we're not heading for a beach. We're heading for Blackhall Rocks!" I cried. We were close enough to the wreck of the *Pelican II* to see scavengers on board trying to strip her of anything useful that was left. They stopped their work to watch us rushing towards them. Some were waving their arms in warning. Others were jumping up and down and cheering. I wished I knew who they were cheering for.

"We are heading for the rocks, but we are not going to run *on to* them," my father said. He crossed the rail and called down to his lieutenant. "Ready to lower all sails?"

"Ready, Captain!" Walsh replied.

The pirate ship was almost touching the stern of the *Hawk*. A few of the men had drawn pistols and held them ready. They could easily have shot me, but shooting the helmsman would not have saved us from the shore. They were calling. "Port, helmsman! Turn to port, or we'll shoot!" I kept my nerve and held my course.

A mast was attached to the front of the black ship, pointing forward like a knight's lance. I know now that it's called a bowsprit. At that moment, I could see it was hovering over our stern and a pirate was beginning to climb along it on all fours, as agile as a barn rat. He had a pistol in his belt and a knife between his teeth, and he would reach me before the *Hawk* reached shore. He'd stab me, then hold back anyone else with his pistol. He'd save our ship from grounding and everything would be lost.

I couldn't let go of the tiller that was straining under my grip from some powerful current. I could only look back in horror as he crawled nearer.

Suddenly Meg raced past me and stood on the stern rail just a hand's-breadth from our attacker. He stopped, suddenly uncertain. He needed both hands to cling to the bowsprit and couldn't use his weapons till he landed on our deck. Meg balanced herself, swung the fish from behind her back and smashed the man in the face.

I had a brief glimpse of blood where his mouth had been cut with his own knife. He screamed in pain, the knife fell into the sea and he clutched at his face. Moments later the black ship rocked and he tumbled into the sea.

Meg's arms waved wildly as she tried not to overbalance. Father grabbed her shirt and pulled her back on to the deck. She was almost knocked out by the fall and sprawled there groaning. Father had no time to tend to her. He shouted, "When I say 'Now!' I want you to throw the tiller as far to port as you can, and as quickly."

He stepped to the deck rail and cried, "Ready, Master Walsh?"

"Aye, Captain."

I saw splinters fly from the rail next to his hand as pirate pistols shot at him. Each puff of pistol smoke was followed a moment later by the crack of the shot. He looked back at our pursuers with contempt.

The wreck of the *Pelican II* was so close I could see the nails in the planks. Father cried, "Now!"

The sails clattered to the deck and I swung the rudder as hard as I could. The effect was like a horse suddenly refusing to take a jump at the last moment and digging in its hooves. Everyone and everything was thrown sideways. The ship rolled dangerously, but the huge weight of the coal kept her from turning over.

The pirate ship, on the other hand, was still under full sail. I picked myself up from the deck in time to see startled faces rush past us and hit the wreck of the *Pelican II* like a plough hits a boulder.

They were close enough for me to hear the cries as the crew were flung from their perches on the rigging and landed on the deck, or in the sea. The old black timbers took the blow worse than the new *Pelican II* had. The pirate ship seemed to shiver into dusty fragments. One of its cannons was thrown off an upper deck, crashed through the lower deck and probably didn't stop till it hit the sea bed.

My father took the tiller from my hands and said breathlessly, "There's a current here that will carry us clear of the rocks on this ebb tide."

He was right. Slowly we drifted away from the wreckage on the shore while our crew began furling some of the sails and preparing to hoist others. When the order was given, a small sail was raised and filled with a friendly breeze to carry us back out to sea.

There was a curious noise coming from the shore. I looked back to see the scavengers on the wreck of the *Pelican II* cheering and throwing their caps in the air.

Suddenly a deck hand from the *Hawk* cried, "Three cheers for Captain Marsden! Hip! Hip!"

There was a roar of "Hurray!" that was louder than I'd have believed twenty men could make. Then I realized that the loudest cheer was coming from my own throat.

As the last cheer faded over the grey-green waves I heard just one voice complaining. "What about me?"

Her small pointed face looked up from the deck, the expression as fierce as I'd ever seen it. Her chestnut hair was falling free of its ribbon and blowing wildly. "Did you say something, Meg?"

"I said, what do you miserable crew want for dinner? The biggest salmon in the barrel has just gone overboard!"

"You'd better go and get it, then, hadn't you?" I said.

She bared her teeth in rage, as I knew she would. But out of the corner of my eye, I thought I saw something as rare as snow in August.

I'll swear I saw my father smile.

CHAPTER SEVEN

"To bring thee to the gallows"

We sailed on down the east coast of England past bleak cliffs and busy ports. We left behind the alum mines at a place my father called Hummersea Scar and saw the sun setting through the ancient shell of Whitby Abbey, ruined by the Queen's father Henry VIII.

The crew gathered to eat Meg's fish stew. The men were in a happy mood and even playful. "This stew's good, girl," a withered old sailor said.

"Who says a woman on a ship's unlucky?" another asked.

"It's true," someone muttered. "It's a fact."

"Ah!" the old man cut in. "But did you know that a storm can be calmed by the sight of a naked woman? That's why the finest ships have a statue of one carved on the bow."

Meg paused with a ladle in her hand and glared at the men, who were laughing. "Careful," Master Walsh said, "she's deadly with a wet salmon!"

Meg tried hard to look angry, but her eyes betrayed her. Only Miles Glub failed to join in the laughter. His mouth smiled, but his eyes were cold.

"I want more food," he demanded.

"You'll have to ask the captain," said Meg.

He rolled towards her with his empty bowl and wiped

his soft mouth on his sleeve. "I ask no one. My money bought this ship."

Meg looked at him thoughtfully. "That's the sort of thing Thomas Doughty said on board the *Swan*, didn't he?"

"Aye," someone chuckled, "and look what happened to him!"

"Yes, look what happened to him," the old sailor said.

"What *did* happen to him?" a deck hand asked.

"I don't rightly know. Captain Marsden was telling us the story when those pirate fellows interrupted."

"That's right! It's bad manners interrupting like that. They deserved everything they got."

"Aye! A smack in the mouth with a wet salmon!"

I turned to my father, who had come down to join us on the main deck. "So what did happen to Thomas Doughty, father? Will the same thing happen to Master Glub?"

"You never know," he replied, and sat down to finish his story . . .

SIR JAMES MARSDEN'S STORY

Back at Blackhall Rocks I told you about keeping the bottom of your ship clean. Well, when you sail through the tropics, the weed and the barnacles grow like a beard till you can hardly move.

Drake took every chance he had to beach the ships and scrape them clean. That was when my captain, Geordie Milburn, had a great tragedy. When we pulled his *Swan* on to the beach, he saw she was beyond repair. The crew scraped down the hull and found it was the weed that was holding her together. Drake ordered her to be burned –

that way the ironwork could be saved and used on the ships that were left.

She made a fine bonfire and the natives of the region came from miles around to see it. They were friendly enough, you understand, and they danced around the fire. It was a party to them. Our men caught the spirit of it and joined in. All except Geordie, that is. I found him sitting at the edge of the forest, his face as hard as ebony.

"I loved that ship, James," he said.

"You'll get another. When Drake returns with his ships filled with treasure, you can have your own fleet."

He tried to speak, but seemed to be swallowing tears – not that a man like Geordie Milburn would cry, of course. I put an arm around his shoulder and sat with him till the flames died and a rainstorm turned his ship into a smoking black skeleton. We sat under the shelter of the huge tree and watched.

That was when Francis Drake chose to come over and talk to Geordie. He picked the wrong time and the wrong man for what he had to say.

He had a sheet of paper resting on a smooth piece of wood and started to draw the scene in front of us. Drake was a wonderful artist and made sketches of the places we visited whenever he could. I watched in awe as the bleak scene took shape on his paper.

"Captain Milburn," he said at last, "you've had the pleasure of Thomas Doughty's company aboard your ship for the past few weeks. Has he given you any trouble?"

"He is arrogant and tries to demand special treatment because he is a gentleman and I am not."

Drake began to add images of the crew sifting through the charred bones of the *Swan*. "And does Doughty say anything about *me*?"

"No, sir."

"Listen, Milburn, I want to put the man on trial. I want a witness to give evidence that he has been stirring the men into mutiny against me."

"But he hasn't."

Drake sighed. "You could *say* that he has," he said softly.

Geordie jumped to his feet and his lips were pinched white with fury. "You want me to lie. Is that it?"

"We need to get rid of Doughty," Drake said. "'*I will rid evil beasts out of this land.*'"

"You are the son of a preacher," Geordie said, "and you like to quote the Bible, Captain Drake. I don't know much of the Bible, but I do know the line, '*Thou shalt not bear false witness.*' Is that right?" My friend didn't wait for an answer, but went on, "Don't ever ask me to put an innocent man's head in a noose, just because you dislike him."

Drake looked at me, raised his eyebrows and shrugged. "He's a good man, your captain."

I hurried after Geordie and caught him at the water's edge. We had unloaded everything from the *Swan* on to the *Christopher* and that's the ship we rowed back to. My captain never looked round once. "Drake is a clever man and a great leader. But never trust him, James. He will lie and twist words and twist men's minds."

"He won't twist your words, Geordie," I said.

"Then he'll find someone else. Doughty is a dead man."

Thomas Doughty had to come on the *Christopher* with us, now that the *Swan* was burned. We sailed south into danger from unfriendly Indians and a cruel winter. We were still looking for the passage round the southern tip of America and still landing regularly to refill our water, to hunt for fresh meat and collect fruit.

Mostly the Indians kept away from us, but in June a band attacked us with arrows and killed two of our men. We beached the ships on a sandy island just off the coast and started to clean them. Two more were broken up for the firewood we needed so desperately. We hardly saw the sun, and most days it snowed.

That was when Drake decided to make his move against Doughty.

He called everyone to a shelter we'd built on the beach. "My friends, we are suffering from this weather. We have lost good sailors to Indian attacks. But now we are facing the greatest danger of all. We are under attack from traitors in our own crew! One man has sharpened his tongue like a serpent, and adder's poison is under his lips."

The men looked around nervously, wondering who was being accused. Of course you always wonder if he means *you*. And it's such a relief when you find you are not the suspect! "There are certain *gentlemen* on this voyage who would like to see it fail. *Gentlemen* who would like to take the treasure and the glory for themselves."

He spat out the word "gentlemen" as if it were a worm-eaten apple in his mouth. Then we stopped looking at one another and turned to look at Thomas Doughty. Drake sat on a log and announced, "I am the judge and I have appointed forty of you as the jury." He read the list of men he wanted as jury. My name was on the list. I took a seat on a bench that had been taken from one of the ships we had burned and faced Drake.

"Step forward, Thomas Doughty," Drake said solemnly.

Doughty stood on the beach and faced his judge. "This voyage is made on the command of Queen Elizabeth herself. Any man who plots against me, plots against the

Queen, and that is treason. Do you agree, Thomas Doughty?"

Doughty's thick eyebrows met in a familiar scowl. "But who says the Queen put you in command, Captain Drake?"

"The Queen herself gave me the order."

"Can I see this order?"

"No. It is secret."

Doughty stepped forward and Drake cried, "Hold him! Bind his hands behind his back so my own life will be safe!"

Some of the crew hurried to obey him and the gentleman adventurer was trussed with coarse rope.

For half an hour or more witnesses stepped forward to say that Doughty had tried to lead them in a revolt against Drake's leadership. The men who spoke were the lowest and most lying bilge rats ever to set foot on a ship.

Drake needed someone honest like Geordie Milburn to speak against Doughty. No man like that appeared. Instead he found men like Edward Bright.

Of course we had all been disturbed by a strange incident that took place on the journey across the Atlantic. We had been sailing in clear weather when a sudden darkness fell and a storm hit us. When the storm cleared Drake's ship had vanished. She was lost for thirty-six days. Now Edward Bright explained what had happened. He stepped forward and said that Thomas Doughty had managed it by witchcraft. "He used magical arts – signs and spells – to get rid of you, Captain Drake. I swear I saw him myself!"

Doughty laughed at this and said it was a lie. I think most of us wanted to believe it because it explained that strange storm. Still, Doughty might well have escaped if he hadn't made one careless mistake.

When the last witness had spoken Doughty turned to Drake and said, "You have no written order from the Queen, have you, Drake?"

"I have, but since it is secret, I can't show it to you," said Drake, looking at a clutch of papers in his hand. "Not even her own treasurer Lord Burghley knows about our voyage."

"Of course he knows!" Doughty said, with a harsh laugh. "I told him."

Drake gave a slow, satisfied smile. "Her Majesty wanted this voyage kept secret from Burghley – *especially* from Burghley. Yet *you* told him. You disobeyed a direct order from the Queen." He turned to look at the men chosen to be the jury. "There you are, my comrades. He has accused himself. I think you have enough proof to find the *gentleman* guilty."

Geordie Milburn rose to his feet. "Captain Drake, I hope this is not a matter of Thomas Doughty's death."

Drake shook his head. "No, Master Milburn. You only have to decide if he's guilty or not."

Geordie sat down and we started to discuss the evidence. After Doughty had admitted he'd betrayed the secret of the voyage to Burghley we had to find him guilty.

Drake thanked us, then told the whole crew to follow him to the water's edge while Doughty stayed under guard. "My fellow adventurers, we have a choice. We can execute Doughty, go on with the voyage and return to England with honour and riches. Or we can give up the voyage and go home in shame and poverty. Which is it to be? We cannot sail on with a convicted traitor in our midst."

"You said you wouldn't execute Doughty," Geordie objected.

Drake shook his head sadly. "I meant I wouldn't execute him unless it was the wish of the crew. You wouldn't go against their wishes, would you, Captain Milburn? Let's ask them, shall we? Men – raise your hands if you think Doughty should be executed."

"Where is the Queen's letter giving you the power?" Geordie asked.

Drake took the papers in his hand and glanced through them. He looked up and slapped his forehead. "God's will! Would you believe it? I seem to have left it in my cabin! The very paper I wanted to have and I've left it. Never mind that now, Captain Milburn. Let's have that vote, shall we? All those in favour of seeing Doughty executed?"

The hands rose as thick as the trees in an American forest. I found I had raised my own hand. I saw Geordie Milburn looking at me, disappointed.

Our friendship was never quite as close after that day. He tried to explain later that Drake had played on our greed and stupidity to get rid of Doughty, when the man's only crime was to despise Drake for being lowborn.

"I wasn't being greedy," I said. "I thought he was guilty."

It's true; I was sure Doughty was a traitor and a witch. But I have to admit he died like a gentleman.

He showed no feeling when Drake marched back up the beach towards him and said, "It is the wish of the crew that you should be executed. I will carry out the sentence two days from now. This will give you time to put your affairs in order and prepare your soul to meet your God."

"You are generous, Captain Drake."

"I can shoot you myself, or I can offer you the axe. Which is it to be?"

"The axe is the noblest way to die, Captain Drake. And, after all, I am a gentleman."

"The axe it will be," Drake agreed.

The next day Doughty prayed at a chapel we had set up on the island. Drake knelt alongside his victim and prayed with him. The day after that the two men dined together and from the deck of the *Pelican* we could all hear their laughter.

Doughty was still cheerful after his dinner with Drake as they walked through curtains of snow to the block. He looked at us and said, "May I wish you every success. I hope God smiles on your voyage and brings you safely home. I have prayed for you and for the health of our queen." Then he turned to the executioner. "And I wish you luck too, sir. My neck is so short, I hope your hand is steady."

He wrapped his arms around Drake and called him, "My good captain," before he knelt at the block.

Drake raised the head for us all to see. "This is the end of all traitors."

We all understood what he meant. Anyone else like Doughty would die the same way. Doughty was buried and Drake named the place the Island of True Justice.

"If any man wants to go back to England, let him step forward now," Drake said after the funeral. No one moved. "Then let us get back to the ships. Let us sail into the Pacific and into history. God save the Queen!"

"God save the Queen!" we cheered.

"God save us all," Geordie Milburn murmured.

The winter cold was bitter and men were falling ill every day. "God save us all," I echoed.

CHAPTER EIGHT

"For the close night doth play the runaway"

The crew of the *Hawk* knew all about the hardships of winter at sea. But it was summer and the North Sea was kind to us that week. It was warm enough for some men to sleep on deck, and that's where Miles Glub chose to sleep.

The captain's cabin I shared with my father became suffocating and his snores kept me awake. I decided to try sleeping on the deck myself. I pulled on a shirt, wrapped a blanket round my shoulders and stepped on to the deck. There was a little light from a quarter moon and from lanterns that hung on the masts.

Across the sea other lanterns sparkled like stars as passing ships slipped by. I moved to the bow and looked down at the white foam we made as we slid through the dark water. When Meg spoke I jumped and almost fell forward.

"Good evening, William," she said.

"Meg! What are you doing here?"

"It's too hot in the galley and it stinks of stale food."

"Yes, it's hot in our cabin too."

We watched a small boat rising and falling in the swell. Her crew had anchored for the night. We had enough seamen to give us a night crew and to sail on. "I understand your father better now," Meg said. "He admired Drake and Drake was a harsh judge. Your father copies him."

"He admired Geordie Milburn, and he seemed a reasonable man," I said. "There's more to the story."

"We'll hear it when we get to London." she said.

I hesitated. It was only a moment, but she knew me too well. She knew me so well that even my silences spoke to her.

"You won't be hearing your father's story in London, will you?" she said quietly. When I still didn't reply she went on, "You're planning to leave the ship and find Hugh Richmond, aren't you? You're going to join his theatre company."

"Yes."

"Don't you care what happens to Marsden Hall?"

"Of course."

"But you think your father can save it from Miles Glub without your help, is that it?"

"Father's at home on board a ship. He's a good captain. He'll get to Plymouth and claim his money without my help," I said.

"Your mother will miss you. And your grandparents and your Great-Uncle George."

"I'll come home one day."

Her pale face seemed to glow in the moonlight and her large eyes looked sad. "And I'd . . ."

"What?"

She turned her face away from me. "I'd . . . like to see Hugh Richmond again. We'll have time while the *Hawk*'s unloading in London. Take me with you."

"*Just* to see Hugh."

"Just to see Hugh," she said. "What did you think I meant?"

"Nothing."

The breeze off the sea was cool so I huddled into my blanket and turned around. There was a large, pale shape drifting across the stern deck. I could see the man on watch drowsing at the tiller. This was something moving behind him. I put a finger to my lips and signalled Meg to follow me towards the stern. We were barefooted and silent.

As we drew nearer we were able to creep up two steps and peer on to the deck. The large shape had to be Miles Glub. He was taking a lantern off the stern, and holding his handkerchief in front of it. He raised the handkerchief three times so the light would seem to flash on and off three times to anyone following the *Hawk*.

"It's a signal," I told Meg.

"Thank you for explaining that," she said. "There *are* times when I need to be reminded how stupid I am."

Meg has a sharp tongue when she has been upset. I didn't understand what I'd said or done to upset her, but at that moment it wasn't important. "What is it?"

"A seagull, perhaps?"

"Probably a ship."

She sighed. "Of course it's a *ship*! Sometimes you have all the humour of . . . of . . . of your *father*."

She really was upset. "We can't go on to the stern deck to look," I pointed out.

"No, but we can look over the sides. You take the port and I'll take the starboard,' she suggested.

I collided with her in the shadow of the cabin. "Port is left," she snapped. "How many times do I have to tell you?"

I leaned as far over the port rail as I could and looked back. There were lanterns of three ships in sight. Suddenly one flickered and appeared to go out, then came back on.

It happened three times. I heard Glub's heavy tread on the deck above me and shrank into a shadow.

He lumbered down the steps saying, "Goodnight, watchman," stopped at the bottom and squinted into the shadows where I was crouching.

"What are you doing there?" he asked.

"Looking for somewhere cool to sleep," I said.

"I thought *gentlemen* slept in cabins. Only commoners like me sleep on the deck."

"No, sir."

"Don't be so unfriendly, young Will. When I take Marsden Manor, I'll make sure there's a space for you. I promise! It's only your father I want to ruin."

"Why?"

"Why did Drake want to destroy Doughty, eh?"

"Spite and jealousy," I said.

"There you are! As Drake would have said, '*Blessed are the meek for they shall inherit the earth. The wicked have drawn out the sword to cast down the poor and needy. But their sword shall enter into their own heart.*'"

"You aren't poor or needy," I said.

He rolled across the deck towards me. "Your family will be when I've finished with them."

His head loomed over me like the pig's bladder I used to play football with as a child. I wanted to take out my knife and burst the ugly, bloated thing. He seemed to read my thoughts. "Wouldn't it be simple to kill me and throw me over the side, eh, young Will?"

"Yes."

"Your father would, if he had the chance. That's why I sleep with the crew. For safety."

He walked away towards the mast, lowered himself on to the deck and pulled his cloak over him.

Meg was by my side. "Are you still leaving the ship in London?"

"Once my father has Drake's money, Glub is beaten. There's nothing he can do to stop Father getting the silver. Nothing."

Meg looked back. There was only one ship in sight now. "Nothing?" she asked.

Hugh Richmond had told me all about London and I'd pictured it in my mind. But my picture was too small. London amazed me.

We were towed up the crowded river, weaving our way between boats of every size.

St Paul's Church was grand, but the cathedral back home in Durham was finer. Still, every other building in London looked finer and taller than anything I'd seen, even in Newcastle. Some houses were four floors high and some were palaces that made Marsden Hall look like a cottage.

The Tower was solid and threatening. I'd heard stories of what went on in there, and I could sense the death and misery that steeped its stones. But the greatest wonder was the bridge. There were more than twenty arches across the river and buildings covered every inch. They soared above the river, looking as if they could topple at any moment. And, above them all, long poles reached into the sky, each holding the head of a traitor.

We docked at a filthy quay where workers were waiting with shovels to unload our coal. I went up to my father on the stern deck and asked, "Would you mind if I went to visit Hugh Richmond? He gave me his address."

His thin nostrils curled in disgust. "What did your grandfather call him? A peacock, wasn't it?"

"Yes, Father."

"Actors are all rogues anyway. A young gentleman should not be seen in the company of men like him."

"I did promise to visit him if I ever reached London. You wouldn't want me to break a promise, would you?"

"We sail at six o'clock."

"It's just after one o'clock now," I said.

"You may get lost."

"I'll ask my way."

"You may be robbed in the street. London is a dangerous city."

"I'll look after him," Meg said, appearing suddenly from the galley.

"Am I to take it you will be armed with a fresh salmon, girl?"

"No, Sir James. Just my wits."

Father snorted. "And we all know that they are sharper than my son's knife." He looked at us for a moment. Something was troubling him. Something he couldn't put into words. "You will be back for six o'clock?" he asked.

"I'll be back by six o'clock," Meg said carefully.

"Then go now. There's not much for you to do here. The men will want to eat in a tavern, so we don't need your cooking skills."

"Thank you, Sir James," she said, and gave a curtsey.

As we reached the gangplank I picked up a leather bag containing my possessions which I'd stowed there as we docked.

My father said it was bad luck to look back when you leave port. I should not have looked back when I left the ship.

My father was standing at the rail looking over the deck of his ship. His chin was raised and his small beard jutted forward. He was proud of his ship and his sailing ability. But

Miles Glub stood at the rail of the bow deck and was looking at him. That strange smile was fixed on his mouth. He looked like a frog, eyeing a fly that was about to become his next meal. "Goodbye, Father," I said, before Meg tugged at my sleeve and led me into the noisy streets of the city.

It was easy to find Hugh's lodging because it was close to the Globe Theatre where he performed in Master Shakespeare's company. We made our way along the south bank of the river, crushed by crowds in some of the narrow streets, stepping over the beggars who lay on every street corner and deafened by the noise of people arguing, laughing or calling out to sell their goods. There were dozens of churches too, and every other one seemed to be ringing its bells.

Above all the noise we heard an explosion that shook the windows of an inn we were passing. "What was that?" I cried to Meg.

A woman passing by said, "It's the cannon at the Globe. It means there's a play there today."

"Can we see it, Will?" Meg asked.

"Of course," I told her.

"Do you think Hugh will be in it?"

"He's bound to be."

"Then he won't be at home. He'll be getting ready."

"We'd better call at his house to make sure," I said. We rounded a corner into Maiden Lane. The playhouse towered over us. It was octagonal, with a thatched roof. A flag fluttered idly from the top and a boy stood at the entrance calling, "*Merchant of Venice* today, ladies and gentlemen. Come and see William Shakespeare's *Merchant of Venice*!"

Across the road from the Globe a shoemaker had the front shutter of his shop lowered to make a display table.

"Hugh lives above the shoe shop," I reminded Meg and walked towards the side door.

As I reached it the door was pulled open and a man rushed out. He wore a bright green doublet with stripes of gold thread. His ruff was starched as solid as a cartwheel and his velvet hat was decorated with pearls. I'd only seen one man dress as brightly as that before: the man my grandfather called "The Peacock". "Hugh!" I cried.

He stopped. "Will! Meg! You're here! I knew you planned to come to London, but I didn't expect you so soon. You should have written!"

"We didn't have time. The chance came so suddenly," I said.

"No matter," he said, walking quickly towards the playhouse while we struggled to keep pace with him. "The cannon's gone off. I'm late! Hurry!"

"Where are we going?" I asked.

"To see the play, I hope. You do want to see the play?"

"Of course!" Meg laughed.

Hugh had reached the entrance and was pushing past the people who were queuing. "These are my friends!" he explained to the boy who was collecting the money, and dragged us through the door into the acting area. "I am simply wonderful in this play!" he called over his shoulder. "I am Bassanio, the romantic hero. Poor but honest, I win the heart of a rich young woman. My performance brings tears to everyone's eyes. Sometimes it even brings tears to my own!"

Inside the theatre was a raised stage with entrances for the actors through curtains at the back. Above the entrances was a balcony. Hugh jumped on to the stage and beckoned for us to follow him. I looked back and it seemed half of London was looking back at me. Poor people in ragged clothes stood around the platform while the better-dressed ones sat in three levels of galleries round the outside. The richest men and women sat on benches on the stage itself, their jewels dazzling in the sun. It seemed as if they enjoyed being looked at as part of the show.

I hadn't time to stop. Hugh led us through the curtains at the back of the stage into a cool, quiet gloom where men and boys were walking around, apparently talking to the walls. I realized they were reciting their lines, making sure they could remember them.

The boys were putting on wigs and dresses to play the parts of women in the play and some of the older actors were helping them. "I don't need much in the way of costume," Hugh explained. "I'm playing a fashionable young man – which is exactly what I am, of course."

"You are also a *late* young man, Master Richmond," a soft voice said.

I looked into the shadowy doorway. A man stood there. He had a neat beard and long hair swept back from his bald forehead. A gold ring glinted in his ear. But it was his eyes that fascinated me. Large, deep-set, dark eyes that seemed to have all the wisdom of the world in them.

Hugh swung round and placed three fingers against his mouth. "Oh! Master Shakespeare!" he cried. "I am so very sorry. But my friends Meg and Will have come from the north just to see me!"

It wasn't exactly a lie, but it sounded as if we were the reason for his lateness.

Master Shakespeare smiled. "Welcome to my Globe," he said.

CHAPTER NINE

"I wish you all the joy that you can wish"

Hugh went off to add some extra pieces of costume to his fine clothes and Master Shakespeare walked across to us. "Have you been to the theatre before?" he asked.

"I've seen travelling plays," I said. "I saw your *Romeo and Juliet* in Durham."

"One of my first plays," he said. "I wish I had time to rewrite it."

"It was wonderful!" I said.

"Everything can be improved," he answered.

Suddenly Meg said, "Will wants to be an actor."

I blushed. I hadn't expected to meet William Shakespeare so soon and I wasn't ready to present myself for a job with his company. The playwright looked at me. "Then now's your chance," he said.

"Now?"

"That's right. One of the boys has gone sick. He doesn't have any lines, but he is a servant to Lady Portia in the play. He has to walk on stage with the three caskets and then take them off again at the end of the scene. You could do that."

"I could," I said. The excitement made me catch my breath.

He showed me three wooden caskets. One was painted

gold and had glass jewels stuck to it, one was meant to look like silver, and the third dull lead. "First you carry the bench on the stage, then you put the caskets on the bench, gold on the left, silver in the middle and lead on the right. You'll need to dress in Lady Portia's colours. Hugh will show you your costume and I'll tell you when you have to go on stage."

"Yes, sir," I said happily and hurried off to change. Meg sat beside the playwright at the side of the stage. He held a script in his hand, ready to help any actors who'd forgotten their lines. When I was ready, I stood behind him where I could see the stage.

The noise from the audience was incredible. The poor people standing on the ground cracked nuts and ate oranges and shouted to their friends. When the play started they shouted at the actors, calling out advice or threats or sympathy.

I was so wrapped up in Master Shakespeare's tale that I soon forgot that I'd be walking on to that stage. Hugh Richmond was the poor young man called Bassanio. He needed three thousand ducats (Italian coins) to set off and win the heart of the beautiful Portia. Bassanio went to a merchant in Venice, Antonio, to borrow the money, but Antonio had all his money invested in some trading ships.

So, Antonio went to a Jewish moneylender to borrow the money to give to his friend, Bassanio.

The mob hated the Jewish moneylender, Shylock, and howled their hatred whenever he appeared. They seemed to forget that he was only an actor playing a part.

Suddenly William Shakespeare was nudging me. It was my turn to set up the scene in Portia's home.

I wondered what sort of greeting I would get from the audience, but in fact they ignored me. They turned to their friends and started shouting their opinion of the play so far. I set up the three caskets and returned to my place at the side of the stage. I hadn't tripped, or dropped the caskets. It was perfect.

It was also what I wanted to spend the rest of my life doing. Next time I wanted to have some lines to say, but the thrill of walking out on that stage had left me sweating with fear and trembling with terror. I had never felt so alive.

Meg squeezed my arm and whispered, "Well done," then we continued to watch the play. "I'd choose the lead casket," Meg said.

Of course she was right. She could be so smug when she was right that I wanted to duck her smiling face into a bucket of cold water.

Hugh, the hero Bassanio, made the right choice, of course. He won the hand of Portia and her fortune.

I removed the caskets from the stage and the scene returned to Venice. It seemed that Antonio's ships had been wrecked at sea. Shylock wanted his money and Antonio didn't have it.

Meg had gone pale while this scene was acted out. I knew why. "It's just like Marsden Hall, isn't it?" I said.

"Yes. But Bassanio will come back and his rich new wife will pay off the debt," she said.

William Shakespeare looked up at us and smiled happily. "Oh, but Meg, that would be much too easy!"

Sure enough, Shylock said the payment was late and he demanded the forfeit instead. With us we'd lose Marsden Manor. But Antonio stood to lose a pound of his flesh.

There was a terrific court scene and now the audience was watching in total silence. Shylock drew his knife to carve a pound of flesh from Antonio's chest. Then Portia, disguised as a lawyer, said, "Wait!" She said Shylock could take a pound of flesh, but he was not allowed to take one drop of blood! Blood was not in the agreement.

Of course Shylock was defeated. He couldn't take the flesh without spilling blood and he couldn't spill Antonio's blood without being executed himself. The audience cheered wildly as the defeated moneylender wept and staggered off the stage.

There was still a scene where Bassanio and Portia had a celebration and I had to go back on as a servant, in a different-coloured costume, to give them goblets of wine.

The play ended and all the actors stepped forward to bow to the audience. Master Shakespeare thrust me on to the stage to join the others. Hugh took my arm and led me to the front of the stage, where I almost trampled on the toes of some of the rich gentlemen in the audience who sat there clapping politely.

Then the curtains on the balcony opened and a group of musicians started a merry tune. The actors began to dance a lively jig on stage while some of the stage hands passed through the audience with caps to collect extra money.

I found myself being swung round by the actor who had been the tearful Shylock ten minutes before. The audience were clapping and having their own little dances on the ground. Firecrackers were thrown among them to screams of laughter. Suddenly I saw Meg had joined us on the stage and was dancing as wildly as anyone. The wooden platform was drumming under our feet and I was sure it was about to splinter under the violent jigging.

Some of the boy actors who'd played the women's parts threw off their wigs and leapt about in an explosion of fun. I had never been so happy in my life.

And, at that moment, something happened to destroy

the mood. It was as sudden as the storm that overtook us on the road from Wearmouth, but a thousand times more disastrous. First, I sensed that the audience had stopped clapping and that screams of fear were replacing the screams of laughter.

The actors slowed their wild dance to see what was happening. The musicians let their music die and quietness fell over the stage like a suffocating cloak.

On the ground a man lay on his back, his eyes staring sightlessly into the sky. His whole body was quaking, raising a faint cloud of dust around him. And the audience were pushing and straining to get as far away from him as possible.

The theatre began to empty as the crowd burst out through the doors and left the stunned actors on the stage. Meg was the first to move. She jumped down and knelt beside the man. "Fetch a blanket!" she ordered.

Hugh Richmond took off his rich costume cloak and laid it over the trembling shape on the ground.

"It could be the effect of standing in the sun for two hours," said Meg.

William Shakespeare had joined Hugh and looked down. "It could," he said. "But I'm afraid it's more likely to be the sweating sickness."

"The plague?"

"Whatever you call it," he said. "The poor man is finished."

"And so are we," the actor who played Antonio said bleakly.

"What does he mean?" I asked.

The playwright said, "Let's get the poor fellow in the shade and give him some water. We'll call a doctor, but I doubt if he'll be able to save him."

The man was whimpering softly. Hugh and I lifted him and carried him into the shade of the backstage area. Some of the actors were hurrying home without even stopping to change out of their costumes. Meg gave the man some water. It seemed to ease his trembling. His eyes closed and his breathing slowed. He slept.

"London often has bouts of the sweating sickness in the summer," said William Shakespeare. "The Queen and her court leave London to stay free of the disease. But the city's councillors say it spreads faster when people crowd into places like the Globe. I don't know if that's true, but they hate us anyway. They'll use it as an excuse to close us down."

"What will you do?" asked Meg.

"Some of the company will load a wagon with costumes and tour around the country giving shows in tavern yards," said Hugh. "That's what I'll do."

"And I usually go back to my home in Stratford and visit my family," the playwright said. "I'll probably leave early next week."

"The theatre will close?" I asked.

"Oh, yes. It will stay closed until September at the earliest. I'll use the time to write a new play."

My disappointment was almost spilling out of my eyes in the form of tears. I bit my lip to control them. Master Shakespeare sensed it and wrapped an arm around my shoulders. "You looked comfortable when you walked on the stage," he said. "You looked as if you were born to that life. In September I'm sure there'll be a place for you in my company."

"Really?"

"You need training, but I could give you that." He ran

a hand thoughtfully over his short beard. "Come back to Stratford with me. I have business affairs to sort out and you can learn how to do accounts for me."

"I already know!" I said brightly. "I help my father with the accounts for our estate."

"Then that's a fair exchange. You do my accounts and I give you theatre lessons. Meet me at the Grey Horse Tavern tomorrow at sunrise and we'll set off for Stratford."

He rose to his feet and went with Hugh to meet the doctor who had come to attend to the dying man. I felt as if I'd met a wizard and been granted my greatest wish . . . and more.

Meg had a faint smile on her face. "Your dreams have come true, Will," she said.

I was too happy to speak. I managed to nod.

"I may see you again. One day."

"I'll come home to Marsden," I promised. "Next summer, if the theatres close again, I'll come home."

"Perhaps."

"I *will*."

"I mean, *perhaps* Marsden Hall won't be there for you to return to."

"Why wouldn't it? Marsden Hall will always be there."

"You may find your friend Miles Glub is living there," she said in a quiet, level voice. "Your father would have to leave, and your mother would go with him. Wherever she went, I'd go."

"My father will save the house."

"Like Antonio saved his pound of flesh."

I was confused. "Why – yes. Antonio *did* save his pound of flesh," I told her.

"He had to have a lot of help from his friends," she

◆ 87 ◆

said. "If Bassanio had deserted him, or if Portia had not been there, he'd have died."

"And you're saying I'm Bassanio?"

"All I'm saying is that we may not be there when you return to Marsden, Will." She stood up and brushed the dust off her dress. She leaned forward and kissed me lightly on the top of my head. "Good luck, Master Will."

"Meg!" I said. But she had turned and was walking away towards the exit. "Meg! I *have* to go. You can see that, can't you?" She didn't turn, or give any sign that she'd even heard me. "Meg! I'll never get another chance like this."

She went out of the door and disappeared down the street. I was left kneeling on the floor. I was surrounded by the brilliant costumes that looked so fine, but were really quite cheap. The sky was a blue circle above my head and the wooden tower around me still echoed with all the feelings in the world – hatred for Shylock, happiness for the lovers, the real joy of the play and the real horror of the sickness. The whole world was in the Globe. It could all be mine. All I had to do was rise up and follow Master Shakespeare.

I looked round to see the playwright standing over me.

"You don't look too happy, young Will. Are you having second thoughts?"

"No. Acting is all I've ever wanted since I saw those players in Durham."

"But?"

"But – but, if I go to Stratford, then I may lose my home," I said, and I told him the story of Miles Glub and the shipwreck.

"Yes, you are like Bassanio," he chuckled. "He won his dream at the cost of almost losing his friends."

"So what do I do?"

"You *know* what I think. You've seen my play. Dreams can wait. But friends who need you can't always wait."

I stood up wearily. "Goodbye, Master Shakespeare. I'm sorry."

His dark clever eyes shone. "Come back in September, Will. There'll still be a place for you. Your father needs you more than I do. Go to him."

Even Master Shakespeare couldn't have found the words to say how much I thanked him. I turned and ran across the stage and jumped to the ground. "I'll be back!" I cried to Hugh Richmond, and waved as I sped through the theatre door.

I raced through the crowded streets, along the river bank and into the dock area. I was desperate to catch Meg before she told my father I'd left the ship. She was walking up the gangplank when I reached the quay. "Meg!" I called.

She turned slowly. I was sure she would turn and run back down to me and throw her arms around me with joy. She raised one eyebrow. "You took your time," she said coolly. "You're almost late."

"But I almost didn't come back at all! I was going to go to Stratford!"

Her mouth tightened in annoyance. "Don't be stupid, Will. You couldn't have let your father down. Not at a time like this. You'd no more go to Stratford than I'd go to the moon."

"How do you know?"

She didn't answer. She was walking across the deck to where my father was waiting, his small eyes burning with excitement. "For God's sake, hurry!" he cried. "We're going to escape!"

CHAPTER TEN

"Let no such man be trusted"

My father seemed to be enjoying some huge joke with the crew. They scurried around, clearing the decks and fastening the hatches as if they were setting sail at once.

"I thought we were leaving at six o'clock," I said.

"We're leaving at *five*. I was worried that you two wouldn't get back in time," he said.

If I'd had my way I wouldn't have come back at all. "But why?"

"Listen, William. We deliver coal to London, but the shipowner makes extra money by loading a cargo and taking it back north. So I've used the coal money to buy a load of grain to take back. We can sell it for much more than I paid when we get back home."

"But we're going to Plymouth."

"I *know*," he said, beginning to get irritated. "But we need some weight in the bottom of the ship anyway – sailors call it ballast – and it steadies us. Otherwise we'd bob about like a cork."

"And what did you mean when you said we were escaping?" I asked.

"I mean there is still some room in the hold. When Master Glub saw that, he said he could fill it with some goods of his own. He went ashore to buy some good leather to sell to saddlers in Newcastle. While he's gone we'll sail away."

Meg laughed. "You're marooning him the way pirates do! Serves him right!"

"It won't get you free of the debt," I said.

"No, but it will stop him spoiling our trip," said my father. He stooped a little and lowered his voice, although there was no one listening. "Some of the men think we are being followed by another ship – a ship full of Glub's villainous friends."

I remembered the signal lights that had flashed at night. "Then why didn't they attack when they had the chance?" I asked. "We're not armed. They could have taken us at any time."

"No," Meg said. "They'll wait for the return journey, won't they?"

"Will they?"

"Of course they will. That's right, Sir James, isn't it?"

Father looked smug. "It *is*. That way they will get Drake's silver."

"*And* they'll get a ship full of grain," Meg added.

"And they will leave me so poor I will have to give Marsden Hall to Glub. That way he gets *everything*!"

"They could also kidnap you, Will, and your father," Meg went on. "They'd demand a huge ransom for your release, and your family would have to sell off the Marsden Manor lands to buy your freedom."

"And who would buy those lands?" Father asked.

"Miles Glub?" I guessed. "With the treasure he'd stolen from us?"

"Exactly! He would have *all* of Marsden Manor, the Hall and the lands; he'd have my ship and its cargo and Drake's treasure."

At last I began to see his plot. "No wonder he wanted to come along on the journey," I said. "It's a clever plan. How did you work it out? You two must have criminal minds."

Father stuck out his chin as if offended. "As a magistrate I have come across a lot of criminals. I know the way their minds work."

"And I've come across a lot of criminals too," Meg added.

If they were right, we were in terrible danger. Leaving Glub in London gave us a chance, but only a slight one.

A line was thrown on to our bow and we were towed into mid-stream. As we drifted past other ships no one seemed to notice us. But the crew of one ship noticed our passing with some excitement. They pointed and shouted to one another. The ship was a little larger than ours and had at least three cannon that I could see mounted on her decks. A man with a fierce red beard and a purple scar on his cheek looked at us as if we were carrying his life savings away.

No one on the strange ship seemed to know what to do, and they weren't ready to sail, so there was no chance that they could follow us immediately. Of course, they didn't have to, I guessed. They could simply wait off the coast of Durham until we made for home.

We left them behind and the crew looked sullenly after us. It was likely that they'd seen us escape the pirate attack so they wouldn't fall for that trick again. They would come for us and shoot the masts down with their cannon if they had to. We had no defence. We had no chance. Why wasn't my father more worried?

At the mouth of the Thames we cast off from our pilot and raised our sails. The breeze was fresher and cooler today. There would be no sleeping on the deck tonight.

As night fell the ship was pitching and rolling in a heavy sea. Meg struggled to serve supper to the crew. "Don't worry," my father called from his position at the tiller. "The Channel is usually the roughest part of this journey – as the Spanish Armada found to their cost."

"Aye," a deck hand told me, "it's the place where two seas meet."

"Ha!" my father jeered. "You should see the place where two *oceans* meet, my friend! Down off the southern tip of America, the Atlantic meets the Pacific and *that's* a channel that even a great sailor like Drake struggled to pass through."

"Tell us about it, Captain Marsden," someone shouted.

Father looked pleased with himself. He ordered Master Walsh to take the tiller for a while and led the men into the shelter of the bow deck. When we were comfortable on coils of rope he began his story.

SIR JAMES MARSDEN'S STORY

After the execution of Thomas Doughty we set off into the winter seas. Not many men were complaining about Drake now. If they had any objections to his leadership, then they kept them very quiet. Of course, I was loyal to Drake through thick and thin. You would never catch me saying a word against him.

My friend, Captain Geordie Milburn, was not afraid to speak his mind. But he was not the sort of man to lead a mutiny. "Drake is not the best man in England, but he is the best leader we have," he said.

Drake led the surviving ships, the *Pelican*, *Elizabeth* and *Marigold* to the south and, when the winds turned in our favour, he led us through the Strait of Magellan into the Pacific Ocean. First we held a special ceremony: Drake renamed his flagship the *Golden Hinde*, the drum was brought out and a picture of Queen Elizabeth was erected to its beat.

It was the first time I'd seen the drum. It was a dull thing, painted in a faded red with gold decorations. It looked so ordinary that I laughed at William Barrett's fears.

I can't tell you all the strange sights we saw on that journey. There were birds on the deserted islands which walked upright like men. Their wings were no use for flying; they were more like fins for swimming. The birds were black, except for a white patch that stretched from their necks to their feet. And they tasted wonderful. They were quite fearless, so the crews had no trouble clubbing hundreds of them and storing them for the voyage.

It was when we left the island that we ran into seas like mountains of water. By the grace of God, Geordie Milburn and I were serving on the *Golden Hinde* with Drake himself. Because, first, we lost the *Marigold*. She became separated from us and we never saw her again. Then we lost the *Elizabeth*. When her treacherous Captain Wynter became separated from us in a storm, he turned and ran back to England. He made it too!

Of course Wynter made excuses about a sick crew and getting low on food supplies. He even complained that, when we set off, he thought Drake was sailing for Egypt. God's nails, *he* had nothing to complain about! I thought I was only going as far as *London*!

"We're alone," Geordie said one night after supper. "Just the *Golden Hinde*."

"But Drake's her captain. If any man on earth can get us safely home, it's him. He has the luck of the Devil."

"Has he?"

"Oh, yes," I said. "We've been through storms that would sink other ships and found fresh food in time to stop us starving."

Geordie huddled under the blanket on his hammock. He was no longer the handsome, strong young man who'd taken me to London. His cheeks were hollow now, his eyes rimmed with red, and his clothes hung on him like an old man's. He said, "I didn't mean that, James." I thought maybe he was feverish, because he began to speak quickly and he didn't make much sense.

"Maybe Drake doesn't have the *luck* of the Devil. Maybe he has the *blessing* of the Devil. Maybe he's even the Devil himself. He can find his way in these oceans when every star is blotted out of the sky by storms. He laughs at storms. He calls himself the knight of stars and storms. Maybe he's more than that."

"You're accusing Drake of witchcraft!" I said. "That's the charge he brought against Doughty."

"Yes, but what if the storms *were* brewed up by witchcraft? Maybe the witch was Drake, not Doughty!"

"And he accused Doughty to turn suspicion away from himself?"

"And perhaps because Doughty suspected him," Geordie said.

I suddenly realized what that meant. "But, Geordie, *you* suspect him."

"I do."

"Then, aren't *you* in fear of your life?"

"Oh, yes. But at least I'll die honourably, the way Doughty did. When Drake dies, his soul will go straight to the Devil."

I didn't sleep that night. When the lieutenant rapped on our door the next morning I was sure that Geordie must be wrong. Some fever had diseased his brain. Drake was a hero, not a monster.

Captain Drake greeted me warmly as I stepped on to the storm-washed deck. He no more looked a devil than I did.

"Marsden!" he cried. "I think these storms are almost at an end. We are heading into calmer water and we'll make a landing within two days."

In that moment I doubted him. How did he *know*? "Are you sure?"

"I'm a born sailor, Marsden," he smiled. "I feel it in my bones." He took my elbow and led me into the shelter of the mast. "Look after your friend Milburn," he said. "I think the scurvy is taking him. Look into his mouth. If his gums are bleeding, he is in a bad way. There's no cure for it."

"I take a potion the Marsden village wise woman mixed," I said. "I'm not ill."

"Can you spare some for your friend?"

"Of course."

He patted my shoulder and walked away to order a change of course.

That evening the sea became calmer and the wind dropped. The next day we sighted the west coast of America again and headed for it. Drake's feel for the sea was wonderful.

Geordie stayed on the ship while we landed and were met by the native Indians. They seemed friendly enough and welcomed us and gave us gifts.

The next morning we went ashore again to fill our water casks and the Indians were nowhere in sight.

We climbed the beach and headed for the freshwater stream that flowed through thick undergrowth. It was when we lowered the barrels into the water that the

Indians came out of their hiding places and struck at us with a ferocious attack.

We fought our way back to the *Golden Hinde* with swords and shields. It was desperate stuff and I was sure I'd die on that forsaken beach thousands of miles from home. I lived. But the next day we buried two of our men who'd been shot with arrows and another man who had died of scurvy.

"What happened on shore?" Geordie asked me.

"The Indians thought we were Spanish and attacked us. Drake was hit in the cheek with an arrow. He was lucky."

Geordie grinned. "Didn't I say Drake's a lucky man?"

But, when he grinned, I noticed the blood on his gums.

After the funerals the men had those gloomy faces and the heavy-footed tread that they'd had when Doughty was stirring up his mutiny. Drake showed me a chart in his cabin that I had never seen before. "I captured it from a Spanish merchant ship on one of my trips," he told me. He placed a blunt finger on a spot on the coast. "Valparaiso, they call this port. With any luck we'll find some Spanish ships there. The men will cheer up when we have a little Spanish gold in our hold."

As usual, Drake's luck held. When we reached Valparaiso harbour three days later, a galleon sat at anchor in the harbour. Drake called the men on to the deck. "That's a Spanish treasure ship," he said. "Would anyone care to make himself a little richer?"

The men laughed. Their mood was better already. "She has only a handful of men to guard her," said the ship's carpenter, Thomas Moone. "Shall we knock her masts down with shot so she can't escape?"

Drake stroked his beard as if he were thinking seriously about Moone's suggestion. Finally he said, "Moone."

"Yes, sir?"

"If you were a guard on that Spanish ship, what would you do if this ship came at you firing all guns?"

"Fire back, sir."

"And, if she fires back with those huge cannon, what might happen to your head if it were hit by a cannonball?"

"It would bounce off!" someone called.

"Ah, but it might bounce on to the deck and smash the *Golden Hinde*," Drake said. "Now what would those Spanish think if we sailed close to her, said 'Hello' – in Spanish – and asked them to get some wine ready for us?"

The men looked uncertain. Moone said, "They won't be expecting an English ship, that's for sure. The English have never sailed the Pacific, have they?"

The plan was formed quickly and by the time we reached the Spanish galleon we all knew our parts. Moone led the way. He jumped aboard the galleon. Ten of us followed him.

"*Amigo*!" the Spanish guard cried, opening his arms wide to greet Moone.

Moone punched him brutally in the face. When they saw what was happening some of the Spanish guards turned and ran for the safety of the hold, and some dived over the side and swam for the port.

No one disturbed us as we searched the ship. I was the one who took a lantern into the very bottom of the hold and found four boxes. They were too heavy to move and were securely bound with leather and iron. Moone brought tools from the *Golden Hinde* and, after three hours sweating in the stinking dark, we managed to open one.

Even in the weak light of the lanterns the gold was dazzling. No one moved. No one was able to take his eyes off the magical metal. When Moone finally spoke it was in a whisper. "Let's get it back on the *Golden Hinde*," he said.

"It will make a truly 'golden' hind," Drake murmured.

We began moving the gold, one bucketful at a time, across to Drake's flagship. It took us two days' work with little rest. As we sailed away from Valparaiso the Spanish stood on the dock-side and stared at us in horror at their loss. They had never believed an English ship could rob them there.

Drake gave me the charts and told me to set a course northwards again. "Well, Marsden," he said, "how does it feel to be a pirate?"

I shuddered at the thought.

"Oh, but Captain Drake! I'm not! I'm a respectable English citizen. I'm not a pirate."

"You are now, Marsden," he said quietly. "You are now."

CHAPTER ELEVEN

"Soft stillness and the night"

The crew of the *Hawk* rose to go to their hammocks for the night. "Who'd have thought it? Sir James, a local magistrate and he used to be a pirate!"

In the darkness it was difficult to see who'd spoken. Especially when the speaker disguised her voice. The men chuckled and my father spoke over the noise of the ship. "I wasn't a pirate. I was on Her Majesty's business."

"Ah, but no one actually saw Her Majesty's letter, did they? Drake never showed it to Doughty, did he?" a deck hand asked.

"No, but Her Majesty *told* Drake …"

"A likely story," Meg said in her disguised voice again.

The men laughed and went to bed happy. My father marched off to his cabin. I found Meg by the light of a mast lantern. "That was wicked, Meg Lumley."

"It does him no harm," she said. "He needs reminding that he's not perfect when it comes to breaking the law."

"Perhaps."

"Oh, Will, you sound as boring as he does," she said, and she went back to her galley to sleep.

My father was in his hammock by the time I got to our cabin, but still awake. "You don't believe that nonsense about my being a pirate, do you, boy?"

"No, Father."

"Good. Good." He was silent for a long time while

I undressed and climbed into my hammock. Then he said, "I felt sure you wouldn't return from your visit to the theatre."

I hadn't known that. "So, why did you let me go?"

"You're not a prisoner, William. If you had not been prepared to work to save Marsden Hall, you're not fit to be master of it when I die."

"I know, Father."

Again there was a long silence while I listened to the slapping of the waves against the side of the ship and the rushing of spray over the deck. But I knew he was thinking.

"That girl," he said.

"Her name's Meg."

"Yes. Meg." He coughed.

"What about her?"

"Don't get too close to her. Don't get attached."

"Because she's lowborn and I'm a gentleman?" I said. Gentlemen marry as high a class of woman as they can. That way they enrich their family fortunes. Marriage is a way of raising yourself up in the world. I felt bitter that my father was trying to control my feelings as well as my actions. I'd come back to help him save our home. What more did he want?

His answer surprised me. "No. It's nothing to do with her being lowborn, William. I just do not want to see you get too close to *anyone*."

"Why not?"

"People let you down. Sooner or later they let you down. The more you trust them and the more you need them, the more disappointed you are in the end. Trust no one, William."

I thought about this. My mother had been as loyal as any woman could be to this cold man. She had never let

him down. Someone before her had done that to him –
someone *long* before he met her. When he was a young
man.

The cabin was totally dark and I was floating in some
unreal world. But, in the darkness, I could see pictures
forming. Pictures of my father as a young man, and
everything I knew about him. Slowly the pictures began to
form a pattern and I knew the answer. "How did he let
you down?" I asked finally.

I heard him breathing. It was going to be difficult to tell
me this. There was no point in my trying to rush him.
"The *Golden Hinde* sailed up the west coast of America
and conquered all the Spanish opposition we met – on
land and on sea. Her holds were filled with treasure. The
crew had never been so content. We would all be rich, rich
men when we landed in England. But our silver was no use
to us out in the Pacific. We were all glad when Drake beat
his drum and called us to a meeting to tell us it was time
to head home."

I heard a rustling from my father's part of the darkness.
He blew his nose, cleared his throat and went on. Every
word seemed difficult now.

"We never knew what Drake would do next. That's
why he was such a great commander, I suppose. We
cheered at the thought of going home. We groaned at the
thought of heading into those raging storms at the tip of
South America. Then Drake said, 'We won't be going
home the way we came.' Of course we knew what that
meant. We were going to carry on west across the Pacific
to China. We were going to be the first Englishmen ever to
sail around the world. All we had to do was survive."

"And you did, Father."

"Some did," he said. "We sailed to the northern part of

America and landed one last time to clean the weed off the *Golden Hinde*. It was a beautiful place, William, and the Indians were friendly. They sat Drake on a rock and gave him a headdress of feathers. He was a god to them. There was enough land for any man who cared to stay there. And some men did."

"They deserted?"

"Drake was happy to let them go. There would be fewer men to eat rations and drink water on our journey across the Pacific. I was tempted to stay myself."

I knew there was something important he had to tell me. Something about "being let down". I thought I knew what it might be.

"Geordie Milburn stayed, didn't he? He let you down."

"Geordie Milburn stayed," he said with a touch of bitterness. "He let me down."

"But if he was happy …"

"He was the happiest of *all* men, William. Geordie Milburn stayed because he died there. Captain Drake was a good surgeon, you know. He bled Geordie and fed him with herbs, but nothing worked. I was holding my friend's head when he breathed his last. The natives helped us to bury him in a place we called Drake's Bay. He deserted me, William. My best friend left me to cross half the world alone. Everybody lets you down in the end. Never get too fond of anyone, William. Not that Meg girl. No one."

In the silence that followed I expected him to say something else. I don't know what. After a long while I heard him snoring softly. Deep into the night I fell asleep myself. Next morning my father didn't mention Geordie Milburn, or our talk. He never did again.

I stepped on to the deck and the sky had cleared. The cliffs at Dover sparkled a brilliant white in the sun as we ploughed along the south coast of England into a head wind. My father pointed out the places I should know about. "There were white cliffs like that in North America where we landed. That's why Drake called the place New Albion."

Meg listened keenly, always wanting to know more. "Hastings, over there," my father said later. "That's where the Norman duke William landed, and defeated the English king Harold in battle. A wonderful deed. A small raiding force landing in a foreign country and conquering it. Just the sort of thing Drake and I did all the time."

"William the Conqueror," Meg said. "Would you like your son, William, to grow up like that?"

"That's why I named him William," my father said.

I hadn't known that. This was a voyage of discovery in more ways than one.

That night, after supper, we dropped anchor near Portsmouth. Sailing into the wind needed constant changes to the sails and the whole crew working at the same time. When they needed to rest, the *Hawk* had to drop anchor. "We have time to sleep tonight," my father said, studying his charts. "Going back will be much quicker. We'll have the wind behind us and we can sail through the night."

Meg went ashore in the ship's boat to buy some fresh bread and meat for supper. She was rowed through the swarms of ships and boats that made the port even busier than London. When we'd eaten and the ship had been secured for the night, there was still some light in the summer sky.

"Tell us about this treasure, Captain Marsden," a sailor said. "Will there be enough room on the *Hawk* to carry it all?"

"Certainly," my father told him gravely. "The shipful that Drake and I brought back from South America took a week to unload. It was stored at Plymouth while Drake sent gifts to Queen Elizabeth. He was worried that she might have been angry with him."

"Angry? For bringing home a fortune?" I asked.

"We'd been away three years. Things change in that time. Queens change. And the Spanish were furious with Elizabeth. She'd locked away her Catholic cousin, Mary Queen of Scots, and the Spanish wanted her set free. Then her English captain, Drake, had robbed them of a fortune. There was always the chance that Elizabeth would hand Drake over to the Spanish just to keep them quiet."

"But she didn't."

"No, she didn't. She took a huge share of the treasure to the Tower of London for herself. Drake was invited to London to be knighted. That was a slap in the face for the Spanish, of course. He didn't even have to go to her palace. We sailed into the Thames and the Queen came aboard the *Golden Hinde*. It was a wonderful day for us all. There was a feast and huge banners hung across the street in our honour. The plank across to the *Golden Hinde* was so crowded with well-wishers that it collapsed after the Queen crossed it! A hundred people fell in the mud below. No one was hurt; it was all extra sport. She used a sword covered in gold to knight him. The Queen passed the sword to a French ambassador, Marchaumont, to perform the ceremony – it was an added insult to the Spanish."

"Did you see the Queen?" Meg asked.

"See the Queen? We spoke for a long while. Sir Francis – as we had to call him now – told her what a valuable member of his crew I'd been. She wanted to know all about me and Marsden Manor. The Queen knows the Marsden family, of course; my mother had been lady-in-waiting to her mother, Anne Boleyn."

"Yes, but what's she like? Elizabeth."

"Like?"

"What was she wearing?"

"A dress."

"What colour?"

"I can hardly remember the colour. It was encrusted with precious stones so that it shone in the sunlight. It was worth as much as my share of the fortune."

"Her face?" Meg persisted. "Was she beautiful?"

"She is a queen."

"You can have ugly queens," said Meg.

"You'd better not let her hear you say that!" Father cried. "The Queen believes herself to be beautiful. Her teeth are a little on the black side, and the scars on her face a little thickly plastered with white make-up – but she has fine bright eyes."

"Her hair?"

"I don't know."

"Did she *have* any?" someone called. "They say she's as bald as Miles Glub!"

Father glared at the man. "Her Majesty wore a fine wig of red hair," he explained. "She is a great lady."

"So why has she never married?" I asked.

"She is married to England," Father said. "Drake told me that's why she supported him against his enemies."

"I thought you were heroes. How could the great Drake have enemies?"

My father cleared his throat and looked a little awkward. "Thomas Doughty's brothers made a fuss, of course. They wanted Drake charged with Doughty's murder. Elizabeth said that was a task for the Chief Constable of England, but at that time there was no Chief Constable. When the Doughty family asked her to appoint one she refused." He sighed. "Not everyone loves a hero. There are a lot of jealous people out there."

"Jealous of your fortune," I said. "What happened to it?"

"When the Queen left the *Golden Hinde* I asked Drake what he meant to spend his money on. He said he was going to buy Buckland Abbey near Plymouth to settle in. It was best to buy land and property, and he told me to do the same. So I went back home to Marsden Manor, and bought as much land as we could. We'd be rich now if it hadn't been for those years of bad harvests."

"And now Miles Glub will take even the Hall itself off you."

My father's face closed into a scowl. "I suffered three years travelling the world to build up my family's fortune. I won't let it go to a man like that."

"But why are we going to Plymouth now?" Meg asked.

"That last night, on the *Golden Hinde*, Drake told us of Queen Elizabeth's dream. She wanted Drake to lead another plundering and raiding expedition. It would be a much bigger venture. There would be men like Raleigh and Hawkins and Frobisher – some of England's greatest sailors. I remember he sat on the foredeck, just as we are now, and said we could all have a share of the fortune. We could either go with him when he set sail the next year, or we could put money into the venture."

"You sailed with Drake again?" I asked.

"Not on that expedition. I'd been away from Marsden Manor too long. I wanted to go home. But Drake smiled at me – I was always his favourite – and he said that for a thousand pounds I could buy a share of the adventure. He'd use the money to fit out a new ship and when he came back I'd get ten thousand pounds in return."

"It was a gamble," a deck hand muttered. "A thousand pounds is a lot of money."

"It was no gamble at all," my father said. His face was smug. "Drake promised that if the expedition failed, I could always claim back my thousand pounds. He signed a paper that says I can have my thousand pounds at any time."

"But Drake's dead," said Master Walsh.

"I'm sure his wife will pay the debt," my father said. He reached inside his doubtlet and pulled out a crumpled piece of parchment. He unfolded it and turned it over. "There is Drake's own signature," he said. "This paper is as good as a purse full of gold or silver. This paper will save Marsden Hall."

"If Miles Glub lets us return safely," I said.

The sailors looked nervously round at the ships that rose and fell on the swell of the sea. They wondered if one might be about to attack.

"Not yet," my father said. "He won't come for us tonight. You can sleep easily."

Of course, no one did.

CHAPTER TWELVE

"Thou stickest a dagger in me"

My father sat astride the horse he had hired in Plymouth. He had taken me with him to meet Drake's widow and Meg had insisted on coming too. "I'll walk if I have to."

My father had learned how useless it was to argue with her. We looked down on the ancient monastery that Drake had turned into his country home. It made Marsden Hall look poor. The farms around were rich with grain, or bright green with grass. The cattle were fat and the barns well stacked with hay from the first mowing of the summer.

"It's a rich land," I said, "so much warmer than our northern counties."

My father frowned. "It is. I only have one worry. The breeze."

I turned my face slowly to each quarter. "There is no breeze," I said.

"Exactly. And without a breeze to blow us home we've lost our gamble anyway. That would be cruel luck. We can survive a storm. We can't survive a calm."

He spurred his horse forward and down the hill to the great house. Servants looked at us curiously. He hadn't packed our best clothes and I suppose we looked a little travel-stained. By the time we reached the courtyard the steward had been warned and he was waiting for us. He was a sturdy man, dressed in the finest black velvet and carrying a sword. No Marsden servant could ever dress so well.

"What do you want?" he asked abruptly.

My father was not the man to be spoken to like that by a servant. "Tell Lady Drake that Sir James Marsden of Marsden Manor in Durham is here to see her."

The steward didn't move. "Lady Drake died four years ago, two years after Sir Francis," the man said.

My father swayed in his saddle and looked as if he would fall from it. "I never heard."

The steward shrugged. "You've had a wasted journey."

"We must still have a claim on the estate!" I whispered to him.

He looked at me gratefully, then back to the servant. "Who owns Buckland now?"

"Sir Francis's brother," the man said. "He's in London at present. His wife, Mistress Elizabeth, is in charge while he's away."

"We must see her."

"You can see her tomorrow," the man said. His face was blank, but something in his eyes told me he was enjoying tormenting my father.

"Tomorrow will be too late. We have only five days to get back to Durham," my father said. He was speaking through clenched teeth in an effort to keep his temper. "I am Sir James Marsden. I sailed with Sir Francis on the *Golden Hinde*. Mistress Elizabeth will be extremely displeased if you do not carry my message to her at once."

"Please," Meg added suddenly.

The man looked at her and smiled faintly. He gave her a small bow. "Yes, Lady Marsden," he said.

The idea that Meg could be taken for his wife made my father splutter, as the steward knew it would, but he turned and entered the house. An ostler came from the stables a few moments later and took our horses. After five minutes in the oven-heat of the courtyard the steward returned. "Mistress Elizabeth will see you now."

We followed the man into the cool passageway. The walls were lined with dark oak and hung with fine pictures. The main hall was lined in the same gloomy wood, but the silver on the sideboard was a rich display of wealth.

My father introduced us and we sat on a bench opposite Drake's sister-in-law. Her pale face was a little too long to be beautiful, but she had fine knowing eyes and a warm smile. "Your brother-in-law may have mentioned me," Father said.

"I'm sorry, Sir James, but your name is not familiar," she answered in a strong Devon accent that I found hard to follow.

"I sailed on the *Golden Hinde* when Sir Francis first went round the world, and then against the Armada."

"What can I do for you?" the woman asked.

"I made a small . . . *investment* with your brother-in-law, and wondered if you would be willing to honour the promise?"

He took the paper from his doublet and spread it on a low table that stood between us and Mistress Elizabeth. It was a curious table. The top was little more than a round slab of wood. But the base it stood on was painted red with fine gold decoration on the side. My father noticed it at the same moment I did. He frowned.

"Ah, yes," Mistress Elizabeth was saying. "My brother-in-law made a lot of arrangements with men like yourself – and women too, if they had money to put into his ventures. Every year we have visits from people with letters of agreement like this."

"And what do you do?" my father asked.

"We tell them what I will tell you, Sir James. I will pay back the sum you loaned Sir Francis."

"The one thousand pounds?"

"The one thousand pounds. I know he promised more, but that money was spent on other ventures."

"No!" my father said quickly. "The thousand pounds will be enough. It will save my family from being evicted on to the roads of Durham County."

The woman smiled in sympathy, but it was clear she didn't want to hear our story. "Come back in three days' time, Sir James, and I will have the money drawn from our bankers in Exeter."

"Three days!" he cried. "No sooner? We can't afford to wait three days!"

The woman spread her hands helplessly. "You didn't think I would keep a thousand pounds in cash in the house, Sir James?"

"I – I – " he stammered. It was something he hadn't thought about. "I'm sorry."

She leaned forward and rested a hand on the paper. "I wish I could help you. There is simply no way I can get a message to Exeter and back in less time. And, of course, the messenger would have to travel with a guard."

My father's face looked bleak and helpless.

I think my own face must have looked the same. Mistress Elizabeth took pity on us. "I have silver in the house, of course. Some plates and cups that we never use. Could you take that instead?"

Meg said, "I am sure Master Glub would never accept

it. He's like Shylock in that play, Will. He'll demand his rightful coinage, or his pound of flesh."

"You're right," I agreed.

"Then what else can I offer you?" Mistress Elizabeth asked.

My father shook his head. He was a defeated man.

Meg leaned forward and touched the round board. I thought at first she was going to pick up Drake's letter. But her hand rested on the wood. "You could give us the table," she said.

My father turned his head slowly. A faint light of hope began to shine in his eyes. "Yes, girl. You're right. We need more than money. We need something more powerful. Money can be stolen from us by Glub."

"We need magic," Meg whispered.

"We need Drake's drum," my father said. I knew he was superstitious, but I couldn't see how a drum could really help us. Even Meg was drawn into his madness and it was no use my arguing with them.

Mistress Elizabeth was puzzled, but said, "I know it was Sir Francis's favourite souvenir from his first trip. He carried it with him on the second adventure and he even took it with him when he fought the Armada. He said it was his good luck talisman."

"It was," my father said.

Mistress Elizabeth shook her head. "It was one of the few things they brought back after his last journey. It's worthless."

"Perhaps," my father said. "But – but *can* we take it? We need all the luck we can gather."

Mistress Elizabeth bowed her head. "If you sailed the world with him, then you deserve it. There are not many of that crew still left alive. Take it, Sir James."

She rose quickly and held out her hand. My father took it and bowed low. "Good luck," she said. She smiled at me and then at Meg. "I hope you get all you wish for."

When Mistress Elizabeth had left the room, we lifted off the circle of wood. As we expected, there was a brown skin stretched over the top of the base. I reached a hand towards it. "Don't beat it!" my father said sharply. "Who knows what forces you may release?"

I shook my head and simply rested a hand on the top. Maybe I imagined it, but I'll swear I felt it trembling as if a wasp were trapped under that skin.

"It's alive," Meg said.

My father wet his thin lips. "Let's carry it very carefully back to the *Hawk*," he ordered.

The drum was light enough. My father mounted his horse and I passed it up to him. We rode back to Plymouth as quickly as we could. We left the horses at the stable and walked down the quayside to where our ship waited. "Right foot first," my father said as he led the way up the gangplank.

The crew stopped their work to gather round and look. "What you got there, Sir James?" the steersman asked.

"Drake's drum," my father said.

The crew looked on solemnly as if he held Queen Elizabeth's crown in his hands. Some were simply curious, but some of the older ones seemed afraid. I knew how they felt.

"Are we ready to sail, Master Walsh?" my father asked.

"Aye, Sir James. But there's no wind."

My father's mouth turned down in its familiar sour expression. "Are the water casks full?"

"Yes, Captain."

"And is there enough food for our journey back to Wearmouth?"

"Yes, Captain. I bought a fresh barrel of herrings from the quay myself."

"Then have us towed out beyond the breakwater."

The former captain shook his head. "He'll have to row us all the way back to Durham."

My father's temper snapped. "Get us towed out beyond the breakwater. I am ordering you, Lieutenant Walsh. Question my decision again and I'll have you swinging from a yardarm with a rope around your insolent neck!"

Walsh clutched at his neck and hurried to obey the order. Before the hourglass had showed a quarter hour gone we were under way.

The crew stood by under the white glare of the sun, ready to lower the sails. Father took the drum and placed it on the stern deck, next to the tiller.

"What do we do?" Meg asked.

"We wait for Drake to come to our aid," my father said calmly. He looked over the stern, back towards Plymouth. He moved to the rail and looked down to the deck where the men waited. "You should have been here in 1588," he said. "You wouldn't have been worrying about a little wind then. You'd have been worrying about what you could see coming over the horizon."

The men turned and looked across the water that was as calm as a looking glass. "The Armada," said Master Walsh. He turned towards my father. "Did you fight with Drake against the Armada?"

"Of course! Drake couldn't have done great deeds like that without me by his side."

The men looked doubtful, but my father stuck out his

chin proudly. "Tell us about it, Sir James," a deck hand said.

But another grumbled, "He may as well. We won't be going anywhere for a few days in this sort of calm."

SIR JAMES MARSDEN'S STORY

As you know, Mary Queen of Scots was executed in February 1587. Once her head had fallen, all England knew the Spanish would come to avenge her.

The Spanish Catholics thought that God was on their side. Of course, their greatest fear was that the Devil was on the side of Drake. There were warning beacons built along the coasts and defences put up all along the south coast. Even in the north of England we were in a fever, expecting the Spanish to land in the south and march north. I think we knew this would be the greatest battle of all. Greater than the Battle of Hastings.

Queen Elizabeth knew the Spanish plans, of course. Her Secretary of State, Walsingham, had spies everywhere and they reported a huge fleet being built in Spain. They'd be joined by the galleons of Portugal and armed merchant ships from the Mediterranean. Walsingham even knew that this monstrous fleet would sweep up the English Channel and join a fleet of barges that would sail from Flanders. The barges would be packed with tens of thousands of troops.

Queen Elizabeth isn't a woman to sit in London and wait to be dragged off her throne. She sent Drake off to Spain to attack the Armada ships in their harbours. That was the sort of thing the pirate Drake was so good at. He sailed into their harbour at Cadiz and blew some of their best ships out of the water. It set back their plans for 1587. But we knew they'd try again in 1588.

It was clear I wasn't going to be any use sitting in Marsden Manor. I'm like Her Majesty. I believe in being at the heart of the fight. I sailed down to London to see if I could join the defending forces. When we sailed into the Thames everybody was talking about the warship anchored near the Tower. "Drake's on board," they said.

So, of course, I had to visit my old comrade Captain Drake, or Vice-Admiral Sir Francis Drake, as he was by then. If he could repay me the thousand pounds I'd put into his last expedition, I could hire my own group of men and command a force to defend England.

I stepped on board Drake's new ship, *Revenge*. He was inspecting cannon on the deck, turned and saw me. "James Marsden!" he cried. "My old friend! How wonderful to see you. Come and look at these guns; you'll like them."

I'd always thought guns were dangerous, noisy things. They were useful, but I had never admired them the way Sir Francis did. He explained eagerly: "The Spanish take guns from their forts and put them on the ships. They have two large wheels and a carriage that takes up half the deck. They can't move them and they can't reload them quickly. But look at this," he said, slapping a fine brass barrel. "*Behold, I will send a blast upon him, and he shall hear a rumour, and shall return to his own land; and I will cause him to fall by the sword in his own land*'. Second Kings, chapter nineteen, verse seven."

"I know," I said. It seemed wrong to be quoting the Bible when talking about that instrument of death.

Drake explained, "It's on a base of four small wheels. It moves quickly, doesn't take up too much room and the gunners can reload in the wink of an eye. This is what's going to defeat the Spanish."

I smiled. "If it doesn't, Sir Francis, I'll be waiting on the shore to drive them off with soldiers."

He frowned. "On shore? With soldiers? The finest navigator in England and you plan to fight on dry land? What's the matter with you, Marsden?"

"Well, I have no ship," I said. "I was hoping you'd repay my thousand-pound investment so I could arm my own troop of men."

He shook his head. "Come into my cabin, Marsden, and let's talk."

The great man gave some orders for gunnery practice and led me to his quarters. A steward supplied us with wine as we stood at his chart table. "That last trip to the Indies was not a great success, Marsden. For every hundred pounds my supporters put in they only got seventy-five pounds in return."

"But my agreement was different," I said. "You promised to repay my thousand pounds whatever happened."

"I know, Marsden, I know. I'm asking you to leave the money with me. When I've seen off the Spanish Armada, I'll be off on another treasure hunt and I'll bring back the ten thousand I promised. How would you feel about that?"

I felt that my chances of leading a troop of men had gone. "You think you'll do better next time?"

"Maybe. It could be that the Spaniards were better prepared, on that last voyage, or it could be something else. It could be that my luck changed."

"You have always been lucky, Sir Francis," I said.

He turned his dark eyes on me and looked serious. "Of

course, you know that the Spanish believe I am *too* lucky to be a normal man? They say I must be in partnership with the Devil. They call me 'The Pirate' and say I have a spirit that I use to speak to the Devil."

"Like a witch has a hare or a toad or a cat?" I asked.

"Exactly," he said.

"So where is your cat?" I asked.

"They say it is my drum," he said, looking towards the corner of the cabin where the drum sat on a velvet cushion. I couldn't believe I was looking at a demon spirit, but there was something about it. I could feel the power reaching out to me.

"And is it?" I asked.

He gave a curious smile, but didn't answer me directly. "If it was, I'd have had more luck on the last voyage." Suddenly he swung round. "Isn't that right, drum?"

I must admit I jumped a little and expected the thing to reply. Drake turned back to me. "But I do believe in luck, and I do believe there are lucky people and unlucky people. I believe you brought me luck on that journey we took around the world. That's why I want you on board the *Revenge* when we go out to meet the Armada."

"Me? Sail with the English fleet?"

"For *me*, Marsden. And for Her Majesty, of course."

"I had imagined I'd be fighting on land," I said.

He swept a hand over the chart on the table. "The Spanish will never reach the land," he said. "We will destroy them at sea. Me, you . . . and the drum, of course."

"So it does have magic powers?" I asked.

"It is just my lucky charm," he said.

"Is that all?"

"That is all."

"And you don't speak through the drum to the Devil?"

"Marsden. I am a good Christian," he said. He stepped across to the drum, rested his hands on the rim and looked up at me from under his fine brows. "I am a good Christian, but I am also a Vice-Admiral of Her Majesty's fleet, Marsden. I could *command* you to come on *Revenge*. And if you refused, I could have you strapped across the mouth of a loaded cannon and fire it. The gunners have a foolish belief that a cannon works better after it has tasted blood, Marsden."

Drake had never turned his terrible temper on me before, but I could see it rising now as sudden and fierce as a tropical storm. "It would be an honour to serve you, Sir Francis," I said quickly. "I'll go and bring my luggage from the tavern."

"You do that, Marsden. We sail tomorrow."

"Sail to where, Sir Francis?"

"To Plymouth to meet Admiral Howard and the rest of the fleet. Hurry."

Of course, the great Drake did not need to threaten me. I would have been happy to sail against the Armada with him. And I was really happy to let him keep my thousand-pound loan till he could sail against the treasure ships again.

The next morning there was great excitement and I discovered that Queen Elizabeth herself was coming to the dock to wish Drake and his fleet well.

She wore her finest wig and her dress was covered in red rubies and white pearls, the colours of St George's flag. She stood on a platform and spoke to thousands of soldiers and sailors. You've never seen so many people in one place, yet her voice rang clear as a war trumpet. I don't remember her exact words, but they were similar to the speech she made a few days later to the troops at

Tilbury. Luckily, someone wrote them down and I know that speech by heart.

"Let tyrants fear," she cried. "My strength is in the hearts and the love of my people. I have not come among you for my pleasure. I have come in the midst and the heat of battle, to live or die amongst you all. For God, my kingdom and for my people I would lay my honour, and my blood, in the dust. I know I have the body of a weak and feeble woman, but I have the heart and stomach of a king – and a king of *England* too. I scorn the Spanish, or any prince of Europe, who dares to invade the borders of my realm. If I must, then I shall take up arms myself and be your general on the battlefield!"

I thought the crowd would never stop cheering. I'll swear that no king or queen of England was ever loved so much as Elizabeth at that moment. We sailed off that day in high spirits and with fight in our hearts.

It was an easy journey to Plymouth. The winds were warm and friendly. But we all knew those same winds were blowing the Spanish fleet closer and closer. All along the coast there were metal baskets mounted on poles and filled with wood. "The beacons," a sailor told me, "ready to be lit when the Spanish come."

Plymouth was crowded with warships of all sizes. Every one looked in fine shape and ready to sail. Sir Francis spent most of his days with Admiral Howard and his captains, planning their tactics. I was ashore checking that the *Revenge* was properly supplied with water, food and gunpowder.

The whole town was packed with sailors and tradesmen and soldiers and farmers. The tradesmen and farmers tried to overcharge the sailors and soldiers, the soldiers despised the sailors, and the sailors hated anyone who wasn't going to sail out to face that mighty fleet. Yet there was never trouble in the streets between the rivals. The quarrels were forgotten in a common hatred of the Spanish.

And there was no *fear*, only excitement. Every day I managed to find some time to climb up on to the headland called Plymouth Hoe. Half Plymouth seemed to find their way to the top so they could look to the south and catch a first glimpse of the Spanish sails.

It was a smooth, turfed area and a lot of men passed the time playing bowls. I have to say I had spent hours practising on the lawn at Marsden Manor and was something of an expert player myself. All the Devon men were amazed at my skill. Every day some new champion challenged me and every day he was defeated.

Until one afternoon I was told that the greatest player in England was waiting to compete against me. I told them to bring him forward. The crowd around parted, and my opponent was taking off his hat and bowing deeply to me. When he had straightened up, I found I was face to face with Sir Francis Drake. "They tell me you can play a little, Marsden," he said.

"A little," I admitted. I have always been a modest man.

"Then we will play ten games and the winner takes ten pounds from the loser. What do you say, Marsden?"

Of course I said, "Yes."

Drake was not such a good player as I was, but it seemed he had more luck. He won the first four games with some shots that were, frankly, flukes. But I did not give up and won the next four. The crowd were enjoying the contest hugely. When the next game was a draw we agreed that the final game would decide the winner. I was about to bowl when someone cried, "The beacon!"

The crowd that had encircled us ran towards the edge of the Hoe and looked out to sea. Along the coast a brilliant yellow flame stood out against the deep blue of the evening sky. On the sun-hazed horizon was a dark smudge. Even with my sharp eyes I couldn't make out sails or ships, but I knew it was a huge navy. Drake stood alongside me. "One hundred and thirty ships, our spies say."

"Shall we get back to the *Revenge*?" I asked.

"What, and let the Spaniards spoil a good game of bowls?" he laughed. "No, my friend. I want your ten pounds!"

That final game was the one where Drake's luck changed. On the last pitch my wooden bowl headed wide of its target. "Ha!" he cried happily. Yet suddenly the bowl struck a small stone on the ground and turned sharply. It landed perfectly on its target. I had beaten Sir Francis.

"Well played, Marsden," he said briskly. "You have the Devil's own luck. '*The race is not to the swift, . . . nor yet favour to men of skill; but time and chance happeneth to them all.*' Ecclesiastes, chapter nine, verse eleven."

"You are saying I was lucky to win, Sir Francis?"

"I am saying that I'm glad you are sailing with me and not the enemy! Time to get back to the *Revenge*."

As we headed back towards the harbour, I asked, "And the ten-pound wager?"

"Oh, Marsden, I don't carry that much money around with me. I'll pay you some other time," he promised, and carried on down the hill.

All the captains gathered on the deck of Admiral Howard's ship, the *Ark Royal*, and Drake returned to the *Revenge* just after dark. "We need to get out of the harbour before dawn, or the Spanish will catch us like rats in a corner."

He retired to his cabin for half an hour while the crew raised anchor and guided the *Revenge* through the swirling mass of ships that had all put out their lanterns. From time to time we bumped into other English ships in the darkness, but before dawn we were clear of the harbour and waiting for the enemy to arrive.

In fact, we were sitting outside Plymouth, almost exactly where we are now! The sun came up and we saw a mass of Spanish ships, galleons taller than a house with more cannon that the Tower of London. A line of ships two to three miles wide.

I swear I felt my heart swelling up to fill my throat; I thought I heard it beating loud enough for the whole of Plymouth to hear. But then I realized the thumping sound was coming from Drake's cabin. "He's beating the drum," one of the gunners murmured.

But when the cabin door opened, and Drake stepped out, I am sure the beating carried on. Drake's drum was beating itself.

CHAPTER THIRTEEN

"Where the carcasses of many tall ships lie buried"

"Drake never did pay me that ten pounds," my father said mournfully.

"But now you have the drum instead," said Meg, and she climbed the steps towards it.

I am not sure what happened next. This all happened when I was a boy, you understand. Memory is like a conjuror that tricks your mind into remembering things that never happened. So I will tell you what *I* believe happened next – and I'll tell you what Meg Lumley is sure happened next.

I believe a sudden breeze sprang up. It rippled over the skin of the drum and made it rattle. Meg reached the top step at the same moment and stretched out a hand to steady the trembling skin, but slapped it too hard so it boomed.

And Meg's memory? She said the air was as still as the rocks on the shore. The drum started to rattle itself and summoned up the wind. Then the wind blew, then she beat the drum and the wind grew stronger.

Who is right? We have argued for years and neither of us will admit we are wrong. Yet it is true that the journey home had a strange and magical air to it.

The drum rattled and the wind blew – or the wind blew

and the drum rattled – whichever it was, the ship rocked. The crew rose to their feet and moved quickly to unfurl the sails. It was possible that the breeze would die as suddenly as it had sprung up so they hurried to lower every inch of sail. The *Hawk* seemed to spring forward like a greyhound. The wind was from the west and drove along the coast at a wonderful speed.

"We'll make it home with time to spare at this rate!" my father cried as he clutched at the tiller and ordered a sailor to check the speed.

The man dropped a piece of wood in the water at the bow and tried to keep pace with it by moving towards the stern. He was trotting and then running and still it was too fast for him. My father checked his chart as we passed landmarks on the coast and calculated that we'd be in London by midday the next day since we could lower some sail, drop speed a little, and sail safely through the night. He sent some crew below deck to rest so that they could take over later.

Meg went to prepare supper, but came back with her hands stretched in front of her, dripping with slime. Her face was wrinkled with disgust. "The barrel of herring that Master Walsh bought for us is rotten. There are a few fresh ones on top of the barrel to fool a buyer. The ones underneath are so old they've turned to slime."

"I'll take the cost out of his wages," Father said sourly. "Have you anything else?"

"Salt beef and some vegetables from Plymouth. Enough for three days unless we stop and buy something else."

"I don't want to stop," Father said. "If we're not home in three days the men can go hungry."

"They'll be furious," I said.

"Then they can take out their fury on Lieutenant Walsh.

It's his fault. If I'd been Drake, I'd have had the man arrested and forced to spend the rest of the voyage eating nothing but ship's biscuits and water. I have a mind to give him that anyway."

"The ship's biscuits have maggots in them," Meg said.

"All the better for Walsh to eat," Father said.

"No," Meg said, "don't do that! The maggots probably taste better than the salt beef."

The friendly wind had put Father in a good mood. He shouted at Walsh and took pleasure in calling him twenty-five kinds of fool, but he didn't punish the man.

By sunset we were level with a place called Start Point on the charts. My father pointed it out to us. "The Spanish Armada came this way, of course. They were formed into a huge crescent like the shadow of a hawk with great curved wings trailing backwards. Drake's fleet followed the port wing of the Spanish fleet and Admiral Howard was further out to sea following the starboard wing."

"Did Drake sail in and sink them with his cannon?" Meg asked.

My father's mouth turned down. "It was not that easy. We had small, fast ships compared to Spain's lumbering giants. But if we'd come too close, their fire power would have turned ships like the *Revenge* into firewood – very small pieces of firewood at that."

"So you just followed them along this coast?" Meg asked.

"We followed them. From time to time Howard or Drake sent a ship darting in to fire on a galleon, but we didn't do much damage that first day. It was at night that we took our first prize."

"I've never heard of a night battle," Meg said.

"It wasn't exactly a battle," Father told us. "As night

began to fall one of our lookouts spotted a lone Spanish galleon. It had broken a mast and was drifting helpless. But it still had dozens of powerful cannon. If we'd tried to attack, it would have destroyed us."

"But you had half the English fleet behind you," I said. "Between you the galleon should have been captured."

Father looked a little embarrassed. "We didn't have the English fleet behind us, to be honest. We were supposed to hang a lantern over the stern so the other captains could follow us at night and keep together. Drake forgot to hang the lantern and the rest of the fleet sailed past us in the dark. As it got light we found we were alone and within three cable-lengths of the Spanish galleon, *Rosario*."

"Drake fought her alone?"

"No. He persuaded their captain to surrender. The *Rosario* could never catch the rest of the Armada. And when her captain saw it was the dreaded Drake in *Revenge* alongside, he agreed to surrender."

"You let the Armada sail away from you just so you could take one crippled ship? What was the point?" Meg demanded.

My father shrugged awkwardly. "There was a fortune in gold coins and silver plate, of course. Most of it went to the Queen, of course."

"Most of it?"

"Well, some disappeared," he admitted.

"How much 'disappeared'?" I asked.

"About half."

"Half! Did it disappear into Drake's money chests?" Meg asked.

"That's what the other captains accused him of. No one knows for sure."

Meg rested her pointed chin on her fist and thought about it. "Drake didn't forget to hang that lantern over the stern of the *Revenge*, did he? He saw a rich prize and didn't want the rest of the fleet to share it."

"That's a shameful thing to say. That's the sort of thing Captain Frobisher said," my father answered angrily.

Meg shook her head. "Drake was supposed to lead his ships into battle. Instead he abandoned them to do a little robbery of his own. He was nothing but a pirate!"

"He was a hero."

"And a pirate."

My father and Meg glared at one another. "But Drake would soon catch up with the Armada after he'd taken the *Rosario*," I said quickly.

My father sniffed. "Of course he did. Drake was the greatest seaman in the world. He always seemed to know what the wind was going to do next."

Meg touched the drum. "Maybe he knew because he *told* the wind what to do next."

"The Spanish reached Calais on the north coast of France. They wanted to join up with the barges from Flanders. But while they were at anchor we could send fire ships among them and burn them. All we needed was a wind from the right direction."

"And Drake's drum gave it to them, didn't it?" Meg said.

"Drake's *luck* gave it to him. The Spanish blundered about in the darkness, trying to escape the fire ships, and crashed into one another. The next day we sailed into them with our guns firing till our shot lockers were empty. Of course they hit *Revenge* time and time again with massive broadsides, but that didn't stop us attacking. There were times when I was ducking under shot whistling past my head and then jumping over cannonballs rattling under my feet. I kept the gunners supplied with powder and shot, and when we were close enough I picked up a musket and knocked their marksmen out of the rigging. I must have killed fifty Spanish that day with my shooting."

"Fifty?" I gasped.

"Well . . . thirty, anyway," he said. "It was certainly more than twenty. Drake said I could have killed the entire Spanish navy if I'd had enough powder and shot."

"And if they'd stood still long enough for you to shoot them," Meg muttered. My father didn't hear her remark, or at least, he pretended not to.

"What happened to the Spanish?" I asked.

"The wind swung round to the south and drove them into the North Sea. Then they were hit by terrible storms and a lot of them sank. It was the weather that finally ruined the Armada."

"So Drake called up a south wind and then a storm," Meg said. "England was saved by Drake's drum."

"And her sailing heroes," added my father, frowning.

"And heroes – like you, Sir James," Meg said.

"Thank you," he replied stiffly.

Meg walked around the drum and touched it lightly again. "I wish we knew how to use it," she said. "What did Drake do to make it obey?"

Father shook his head. "I often thought I heard him talking in his cabin. When I knocked on the door the talking stopped. And, when I went into the room, there was no one for Drake to talk to."

"What sort of talking?" Meg asked. "Praying like a priest?"

"No. More the way you would talk to a friend."

Meg squatted and brought her face close to the drum. "You're really clever, drum," she said. "You saved England, didn't you? Is that because you hate the Spanish for being Catholics? Is that why you helped Drake? Well, if you are clever enough to save a country, you can do a simple job like saving us, can't you? Keep this steady wind at our backs – and warn us when there's danger."

"This is madness," I said. "You can't talk to a drum! It can't hear you!"

"No. Let her carry on," my father said.

Meg smiled at the drum. "I wish I knew what we could do for you in return."

"You can let it take your soul to hell, Meg," I warned her. "That's what the Spanish said Drake did."

"It's not evil, Will. Magic, but not evil." She turned back to the drum. "We're being hounded by a wicked man called Miles Glub. I have a strange feeling he may be a secret Catholic."

"Meg!" I cried. "You can't tell it lies."

"I thought you said it couldn't hear me," she replied.

"I'm going to my hammock," I said, and left her and my father on the deck with their drum. I was more worried about Glub's friends attacking with knives and pistols than the nonsense about the drum. I slept well and enjoyed the journey the next day. We were in sight of land most of the time and Father showed me some of the navigation skills that Geordie Milburn had taught him, as well as some of the landmarks we'd missed on the journey down.

The next night we passed Dover and began to head north. Luckily the wind had shifted during the night to the south and it was still behind us. Meg looked smug and said, "But of course the wind changed when we wanted it to!"

I looked longingly at the Thames as we wove through the shipping that spilled out into the North Sea. Father could have dropped me in London, and I might have caught Master Shakespeare before he set off for Stratford. Or, perhaps, I could have joined Hugh Richmond and gone on tour around the country with his travelling players. But there was no time to stop and Marsden Hall wasn't saved.

"We don't have Glub's money," I reminded Meg.

"But we have the drum," she said happily.

"I don't think he knows how to play it," I snapped back.

If Glub were going to attack it would be on this home run. We sailed past ports and several times ships came out and followed us. Then they passed us, or headed towards Flanders, or turned into another east-coast port.

He came when we were not expecting him, of course. He would. After all, he probably thought we were armed. He had to catch us asleep and off guard.

He attacked at the same time Drake chose to attack the Rosario. He attacked when the dawn sky was beginning to lighten, although it would be an hour before the sun came up properly.

I was sleeping soundly and woke with a sudden fright. Something was wrong. In my sleep something had happened. I'd wakened, but didn't know why. Then I heard it.

A rattle.

There was something loose in the hold and it was clattering around. Something large, like a cannon, was dangerous if it broke free below decks. But this was small and the rapping it made was quite gentle.

I realized it had a steady beat.

I waited for it to stop again. I expected it would strike the side of the ship and then stop and roll back. Suddenly there was a louder, closer knock that made me jump. Someone was knocking on the door. My heart stopped for a few moments, then I heard Meg cry softly but urgently. "Will! Sir James!"

My father stirred while I thrust my feet to the floor and tried to find my clothes. "What is it?"

"That rattle!" Meg said.

"Something loose in the hold."

"No, it's the drum!"

"Who's playing the drum? It's not even morning yet," I grumbled as I pulled up my breeches and tried to lace them to my doubtlet in the dark.

"No one's playing it!" she said. "It's playing itself."

I stopped and listened. The rattle could well be someone playing a drum. Or it could be the drum rolling around below decks. I pulled open the cabin door and a fresh breeze slapped my face awake. My father followed me a minute later.

The ship was rolling a little in the sea swell. It was probably enough to make the drum topple over and roll around like that.

"Where is it?" my father asked.

"In the fore sail locker, Sir James," Meg told him.

He rubbed his hands a little nervously and lifted the latch on the locker door. The drum had fallen over. It lay there, but it was silent now.

"You've woken us up because the drum fell over," I said.

A pink spot grew in each of Meg's cheeks. "It *hadn't* just fallen over. It was playing itself. You heard it."

"You *imagined* it," I said.

"We heard something, William," my father said.

"It's a warning!" Meg said. Her voice was rising. The crew were starting to come out of the hold where they had been sleeping.

"What is it warning us about?" I said. I have to admit I was jeering at her fears.

"If I knew *that* I wouldn't need to be warned," she said.

My father called to the man who'd spent the night at the tiller, "Where are we?"

"Just past Spurn Head, Sir James. We'll be home by noon at this rate."

"Have you seen any other ships?"

"Nothing, Sir James."

"Climb the mast, William. You'll see further from there," my father ordered.

"It's cold!"

"Come along, boy. Put our minds at rest, then we can get back to our hammocks for another hour's sleep."

I glared at Meg for the trouble she was causing me. She just looked to the horizon and frowned. I struggled up the mast to the crow's-nest. To the west a dark headland loomed up. That must have been Spurn Head. To the north, ahead of us, there was open sea, grey as granite under the pearl sky. I turned to the east and saw the sky streaked with burning scarlet where the sun was soon going to appear. What had father said? "Red sky in the morning – sailors take warning." If he was right, we were due for a storm.

Finally I looked to the south, to where the wide mouth of the Humber River opened into the North Sea. A ship in full sail was coming out of the estuary and turning in our direction. "Ship to stern," I called down.

"How big?"

"Twice the size of the *Hawk*."

"It's a strange time to be sailing," my father was saying as I climbed back down. "He's left the Humber against the tide. He must have a reason for doing that."

"Because he saw us and he's coming after us," said Meg.

"We couldn't see him," I said.

"No," said my father. "But he could have had a lookout on the headland. A signal to that ship and they'd be ready to sail after us. It's a good place. The nearest safe harbour's probably Bridlington, and that's over thirty miles from here. He'll catch us long before that."

"What can we do?"

"We can try to outrun him." My father gave orders for every inch of canvas to be raised and the men ran to obey.

The mainmast of *Hawk* was bending under the strain as she surged forward. But soon we didn't need a lookout in the crow's-nest to tell us there was a ship following in our wake. We could see it from the stern deck now.

"He'd have been aboard before we woke," Meg said. "The drum saved us."

"No, Meg," I said, as the sun broke over the horizon and glinted on the cannon of the ship behind, "even if you think the drum *warned* us, it hasn't *saved* us."

CHAPTER FOURTEEN

"Despair and shuddering fear"

"He won't try to sink us," my father called over the roar of the ocean as *Hawk* struggled to keep ahead of the following ship. "He will try to board us. He believes we have silver on board and he will probably try to kidnap me. But you men should be safe."

"What'll happen to us?" asked a young deck hand called Hatton.

"You'll probably be put in the ship's boat and left to row ashore."

The men began muttering among themselves. "Will we get paid for this trip?" Master Walsh asked.

The men nodded in agreement. "How can I pay you if I lose my ship, my cargo and my freedom?" my father replied.

"You can't," said the lieutenant. He turned to face the men. "We'll just have to make sure Sir James and the *Hawk* stay out of the hands of those villains."

"Aye!" the men cheered.

"How will you do that?" my father asked.

"Why, we'll fight, Sir James. We'll fight!"

My father looked quite proud of the mixed crew of men and boys. "We haven't got a weapon on the ship!" he said.

"Oh, Sir James! You've sailed the world with the

famous Drake. You must know there are a dozen weapons on a ship!" Hatton cried. He picked up a long, heavy pole that was used to push the ship off the quay as she left port. "How would you like to be hit in the belly with this?"

"I wouldn't!" someone laughed.

"Well, that's what's going to happen if any stranger tries to set foot on the *Hawk* without Captain Marsden's permission!"

The men cheered him. Another took a rope and pulley that was used to haul the grain in and out of the hold. "Fasten a hundredweight sack of corn to this, swing it, and you have a weapon that'll knock a man clean overboard."

"He won't hit the water till he's halfway to Flanders," someone agreed.

"And ropes!" I said. I picked up a length of rope. There was a wooden pulley attached to the end. It hummed as I swing it round my head. "David could have knocked Goliath down with this."

"Aye," Master Walsh said, "it's a bit like David and Goliath, this fight. They're the big bully Goliath – but we all know who won that battle, don't we, lads?"

"Yes!" they cheered.

"Sir Francis Drake would have been proud of you," my father said. "The mighty galleons of Spain were sunk by the little ships of England. But it wasn't the cannon inside the ships that won the battle. It was the mighty English hearts inside the sailors!"

The men cheered him wildly. I'd never heard my father give a speech like that. He seemed even to have amazed himself. I turned to Meg. "Where did that speech come from?"

"From Drake himself, by the sound of it."

"Drake's not here," I said.

"No, but his drum is," she said and grinned wickedly. "Sooner or later you're going to have to believe in it, William."

She walked towards the galley. "What are you going to do?" I asked. "It might be safer if you hid below decks till it's all over."

She stopped. Her back was towards me, but she managed to put more expression into the way she stood than most people put into their faces. She turned slowly. "What?"

"I thought – I thought – I was thinking about your safety."

"Thank you," she said. Her green eyes were as cold as the sea beneath the ship. "And did I hide below when we were attacked by pirates?"

"No – but – "

"And if I hadn't helped by beating off that pirate who was about to jump on board, where would you all be now?"

"I know, Meg, but – "

"You may have a little more strength in your body," she said fiercely, "but some of us have a little more sense in our heads."

"You're right," I said.

She jabbed a finger at me. "Come here and use some of those muscles. Help me get the barrel of herrings out of the galley."

I followed behind her like a dog with its tail between its legs. "You aren't going to cook breakfast, are you?"

"Yes!" she said. "As soon as Miles Glub's men land on our deck, I'm going to offer them a meal. One mouthful of the rotten herring and they'll fall dead on the decks."

"I'm *serious*, Meg,"

"And so am I. Remember what Queen Elizabeth said during the Armada crisis? '*I have the body of a weak and feeble woman, but I have the heart and stomach of a king.*'"

"Yes, but Elizabeth never went within fifty miles of the Armada battles. She didn't really mean it. There was never any chance of seeing her blood in the dust, or whatever she said."

"True," Meg said. "She was a middle-aged queen. But I'm not. I'm Meg Lumley. And, like Her Majesty said, I want to live, or die, amongst you all. I really *do*, Will. If you lose this battle and you lose Marsden Hall, then I lose everything I care about too. Please don't try to stop me."

I wondered how I ever dreamed I *could*. I helped her heave the stinking barrel on to the deck. I thought I could see her plan. If she rolled it down the deck as the attackers jumped on board, the barrel would knock them over like skittles. Of course, if the bow of the ship rose on a wave, the barrel would roll back and crush her.

We came out of the galley to find the excited crew had set about inventing new weapons made from anything they could find. I remembered some of the stories Great-Uncle George used to tell me. There was a story about Romans who fought to the death for sport. They were called gladiators, and some of them were armed with a net. I searched through a locker until I came up with a fishing net that we used to catch fresh fish when we came across a shoal.

At first when I threw it, the net hung in the air and landed on my head. I weighted the corners with wooden blocks and found I could throw it quite well.

One of the boys climbed up to the crow's-nest and used a rope to haul up a basket full of iron fittings and wooden blocks that we kept to repair damaged seams on the ship. I climbed to the first step of the mast and looked ahead. There were small villages on the coast, but no landing stage for a ship as large as the *Hawk*, and there was no sign of Bridlington.

To the stern our pursuers had a larger ship with an extra mast. The following wind meant that she was gaining on us by half a mile in every mile we sailed. We could have turned and tried to wriggle away from her, but there was nowhere to run to. My father was right. Our only hope lay in keeping them off the *Hawk* until we reached a harbour where local law officers could protect us.

I stood next to my father at the tiller and watched the strange ship draw closer. There was no doubt now what they meant to do. While a dozen men worked the sails, the ropes and the tiller, another half-dozen stood on the foredeck watching us. They were armed with cutlasses, and pistols were stuck in their belts. They had wound scarves around the lower halves of their faces.

"That's a good sign," my father said calmly.

"I don't see why."

"It's so we can't recognize them. If they planned to murder us and throw us to the fishes, it wouldn't matter if we saw what they looked like."

That made sense. But attacking a ship was still a hanging crime, and they could still turn to murder if their capture plan went wrong.

My father fixed his gaze on the compass and was so unruffled I could believe that he was experienced at sea warfare. I'd always seen him as weak, but now I had to look at him with fresh eyes. He glanced up suddenly and caught me watching him. He gave a small smile. "It is in the heat of battle that the steel of a sword is tested, not in peacetime. And it's in the heat of battle that the steel of a man is tested."

I nodded and returned the smile. "You stand the heat well," I said.

He blinked. "Me? No, no, boy! I meant *you*! You are taking this calmly and bravely – I like to see that in a man."

"A man?"

"Yes, son. A man."

I turned away from him and pretended to tighten a loop on the net I was holding. I didn't want him to see the tears that were pricking my eyes. I was young, and I had the childish idea that men don't cry.

There was a crack from the cannon on the enemy deck but no sound of any shot striking the *Hawk*. "It's just gunpowder. Just a warning in case we didn't know what they are about," my father said. The other ship began to pull alongside and my father looked across at her. "They're going to try to board us from the side. It's a tricky thing to do, especially when you're not a seaman."

"Aren't they sailors, then?" I asked.

Father shook his head. "Glub just collected a few bullies from the gutters of Newcastle. Look at their clothes – sailors don't wear doublets and hose. He's got sailors to run the ship, but a gang of roughs to do his fighting. They may be a problem in a dark Newcastle alleyway, but they'll not find it so easy at sea. My men are real sailors."

The bullies had gathered on the rail at the side of the ship and were waiting for the ships to come close enough to jump across. Their mouths were hidden, but I could see their eyes now, and some of them looked uncertain, or even afraid. A man who missed his jump could drown, or be crushed between the hulls.

The enemy had a larger ship and the men would have to

◆ 141 ◆

jump down on to our deck. The crew of the *Hawk* had waited quietly, but now they could see their attackers, they began to jeer at them. "Come aboard, shipmates!" Master Walsh called. "We have a welcome ready for you!"

At the stern their captain was at the tiller. As he drew level my father looked across and gave a small bow. "You are a good sailor, sir, but a foolish man. You will hang for this."

The captain turned away and suddenly swung the tiller so his ship crashed into the side of ours. The movement caught the waiting attackers by surprise. Three were flung on to our deck and landed on their hands and knees. Their weapons clattered over the planks, and our crew were on to them before they could get to their feet. They had no chance against our men, who moved easily over the rolling ship as they had been doing for years.

The bruised and beaten attackers were tied with expert knots and fastened to the foremast. My father turned away from the other ship and took the wind from his sails. "That's the way Drake taught me to fight the big Spanish galleons," he said. "The ship that has the wind has the advantage."

Now, instead of ploughing into the waves, they were striking us from the side. The other ship managed to come alongside again, but she was rising and falling so that one moment the waiting men had to jump down from the height of a house top and the next they were below us.

One man tried to judge his jump for when the ships were level. As he leapt, our ship dropped into the trough of a wave and he found it falling faster than he was. Suddenly it began to rise again and his feet hit the deck with a terrible sound. He lay screaming with the pain of a broken ankle. The crew of the *Hawk* were almost gentle as they bound his legs and carried him over to his friends.

A sailor from the other ship held the attackers back while he threw a light anchor towards us. It caught under the side rail and he quickly lashed it to his own vessel. Now the ships were tied together, it would be easier for the men to jump across. The enemy captain turned his ship out of the wave troughs and dragged out lighter vessel with it. "Cut that rope!" my father cried urgently.

The crew of the *Hawk* hurried to obey, but they were too late. A tall, heavy man stood on the rail and steadied himself to jump across. Master Walsh lunged at him with the long pole, but the man stroked it with his cutlass and it snapped. He bent his knees slightly and prepared to jump down. He landed lightly on the deck. A heavy sack of corn swung at him from the end of a gantry. He saw it at the last moment and ducked.

He waved his cutlass at the crew of the *Hawk* and they backed away. He stepped towards his friends who were lashed to the mast and raised his cutlass to cut their bonds. Suddenly a heavy wooden block dropped from the crow's-nest and hit him on the shoulder. He roared with pain, dropped his sword and looked up to see where it had come from. That was a mistake, for the next block caught him full in the face. Even through the mask I could see the blood spurting from his burst nose. He fell, dazed, and was quickly pounced on with ropes.

There were just two others waiting to jump. One carried pistols, and it was clear that he was not going to wait to be set upon by men with lumps of wood and ropes. He made a large jump to land safely on the deck. But while he was still in the air, I heard Meg cry, "Now!"

With the help of the cabin boy she pushed over the barrel of rotten fish, and a wave of grey slime shot across the deck. The man landed in the slime and skidded. As his elbows hit the deck the pistols exploded and the shots went harmlessly into the air. Then he kept sliding till he reached the mast and met it with his head. As the ships rolled a little, the man slid towards the stern, then back towards the bows. A deck hand grabbed him and slid him across to Lieutenant Walsh, who had him tied up.

The last bully stood on the rail, his eyes filled with fear. I took my net and walked carefully over the stinking fish slime towards him. "One more fish to catch, lads!" I cried. The crew cheered.

The man looked at the net and dropped back on to his ship. "You're mad. You're all mad!" Suddenly he pointed at me. "Fighting with nets isn't fair," he shouted. A wooden block from the crow's-nest exploded next to his foot. He turned and ran to the nearest cabin and disappeared.

Our crew began to bundle the attackers towards the rail and heave them on to their own ship. The man with the broken ankle screamed, but his friends did nothing to help him. They were all too shaken to have any fight left. The large attacker who'd knocked himself out was too heavy to carry. "Leave him!" my father ordered. "We'll need a witness to bring these pirates to justice."

Lieutenant Walsh used a fallen cutlass to slice the rope that bound the ships together. As they drifted apart, my father called to the captain opposite, "I'll have you know that I fought with Drake. I defeated Spanish galleons and I will defeat you if you wish to try again."

As the crew of the *Hawk* cheered, the sour-faced captain swung his ship away. There was a cabin built into the stern and, just for an instant, I saw a face at the window. It was a face that I would recognize anywhere, at any time. It was topped by a shining bald dome and the mouth was twisted into a fixed smile.

"Miles Glub's on that ship, Father!" I said.

My father's thin, gloomy face lightened. "Then he is as guilty as any of the others of piracy. I will place the rope around his neck myself when we get back to Marsden Manor."

CHAPTER FIFTEEN

"Therefore thou must be hanged"

The crew were excited by the victory and eager to tell one another the part they'd played.

The boy in the crow's-nest claimed to be the real hero, but some of the crew thought Meg's use of the fish slime had been the secret weapon that won the battle. My father handed the tiller to me and, leaning on the rail, called them to order. "We won because we were sailors fighting on our own favourite battle-field. But we still have to get this ship safely home. So get that deck swabbed down before we choke on the stench, and get the ship tidied up. I'm not going into Wearmouth with my decks covered in splintered wood and rusting cutlasses."

"What shall we do with the prisoner?" someone asked.

"Bring him to me. We'll have his trial as soon as that deck is cleared."

The idea excited the crew again, but they hurried to obey orders. Leather buckets were lowered into the sea to swill the slime off the decks.

The attacking ship was pulling ahead of us fast. Meg joined my father and me on the stern deck. "Do you think he'll try again?" she asked.

"He may want to, but I can't see his men agreeing to it.

Glub will just have to hope that we don't deliver the money on time."

"And we haven't got it yet," I said.

"We'll get five hundred pounds for this cargo of wheat," my father said.

"And if we can prove he was mixed up in this attack, we can bargain with his life," Meg said.

"No. This is a debt. I would not hang a man just to escape paying him his thousand pounds. That is not justice, Meg Lumley."

"It'll save Marsden Hall!"

My father's face was harsh. "I am a gentleman," he said coldly. "If I use back-alley methods like Glub and his friends, I don't deserve Marsden Hall to be saved."

Meg looked astonished and disappointed. "Francis Drake wouldn't have minded," she said.

My father shrugged. "As Thomas Doughty said, Sir Francis was not a *true* gentleman. He was in the habit of breaking the laws of God and man when it suited him. I admired Drake, but I do not want to copy him."

"I'll remember that when Miles Glub throws us out of Marsden Hall," said Meg. "Sir James Marsden and Thomas Doughty were losers, but at least they were gentlemen."

She turned on her heel and walked back to the galley. The slamming door echoed round the ship like a cannon shot.

When the deck had been cleared, the prisoner was lifted up and tied to the mast. The crew gathered round and Father handed the tiller to Master Walsh while we held our trial.

The man's face was hidden under a tangled mat of ginger beard, which didn't quite cover a purple scar that stretched from his top lip to the corner of his eye. His coat was made from fine, dark-blue cloth, but now it was stained and ruined with the fish slime. A trickle of blood ran from his scalp where his head had struck the mast and his eyes were still dazed.

"What is your name?" my father asked.

"Mind your own business," the man growled. His voice had the same strong Newcastle accent as Miles Glub.

"But it is my business. You attacked my ship!"

"I never."

"You jumped aboard waving two pistols! You're not going to try to deny it!" I cried. My father glared at me, his look telling me it was not my place to interrupt.

The man turned his red-rimmed eyes towards me. "We wanted to pay a friendly visit," he said. "We had a load of fish from Hull. We thought you might like to buy some."

The crew laughed at his nerve, but my father was boiling with rage. "Who is your captain?"

The man was relaxing now. He scratched his head lightly and looked at the blood on his fingers. "Dear me, I seem to have forgotten. Must have been the knock on the head."

"Who hired you to attack us?"

"I can't remember *his* name either! Isn't it terrible what a blow on the head will do?"

"Describe the man."

"Small – very small."

"Bald?"

"No. Hair right down to his waist."

My father's fists were clenched tight and his knuckles white. He turned away and called four of the strongest crew members to join him in a huddle in the shelter of the foredeck. The man smiled at me. "Tell your captain that it's against the law to kidnap a man – especially a poor fish-seller. Tell him I want to be put ashore at the next port. If he does that, I won't report him."

"It's not a good idea to anger him any more," I warned. "He has a fierce temper."

"Oh, dear. Look at me! I'm shaking with fear," he said, and gave a rumbling laugh.

My father returned from his conference with the four crew members. Two of them untied the prisoner and held him. Father ordered the sails to be furled and the ship to drop anchor.

As the ship drifted to a halt one of the crew climbed the mast with a rope, threw it over a spar and lowered both ends to the deck. "What's happening?" Meg asked as she came out of the galley. "Why have we stopped moving?"

"I don't know," I said.

A sailor tied a noose in one end of the rope over the spar. My father held the other end. When he tugged it the noose rose in the air. The prisoner had his hands tied in front of him and the noose placed around his neck.

The cabin boy had taken Drake's drum out of the sail locker. It stood on the deck and now he rattled it in a long, chattering death roll.

"I hereby sentence you to hang," my father said coldly. "Have you anything to say before the sentence is carried out?"

The drum stopped. The only sound was the lapping of the sea against the hull. The prisoner let a slow grin cross his face. "Hang me, Magistrate Marsden. Go on, you haven't got the guts."

"Ah!" my father cried. "You forget who hired you, yet you know *my* name."

The man snorted. "I know you are a man of the law.

You wouldn't hang anyone without a proper trial. You have to have a jury and witnesses."

Father turned to the crew. "Drake had a similar problem when he executed Doughty. You remember, he asked his men for their verdict. So now, men, I ask you: do you want to see this man hang?"

"Yes!" came the reply, with a roar.

"No!" Meg cried. "You can't do that! He deserves a proper trial!"

"I am captain of this ship, just as Drake was captain of the *Golden Hinde*. He executed Doughty, though no one said that he had the right to do it."

"Drake was a pirate. You're not," she said fiercely.

"Quiet, girl. I know what I'm doing." He looked at the prisoner. "What is your name?"

"Her Majesty Queen Elizabeth," the man sneered.

Father nodded at the men who held the prisoner. They lifted him on to the rail. "Careful!" the man cried. "I could have an accident. Ha! You won't hang me, Marsden, and you don't even scare me."

"Who sent you?" Father asked calmly.

"My dad, Henry the Eighth."

My father gave a tug on the rope and it tightened around the man's neck, making the purple scar stand out more vividly. He took a step towards him. "Are you going to answer my questions?"

The man spat full into my father's face. Father stretched out a hand and pushed his knee. For a few moments he struggled to keep his balance. His mouth gaped and he gave a huge scream as he toppled over the side.

I heard Meg sob. While the man was still falling and screaming my father let go of the rope. The scream stopped as the man hit the water.

We rushed to the side and watched as his head broke water. "I can't swim!" he shrieked.

"Hold on to the rope around your neck and we'll haul you up," Father told him.

The man was slowly drawn up. He fell on to the deck, too weak to rise. "I've never been – I've never – never been so – so frightened! I thought – thought – you hang – really was – really. God's teeth – frightened."

"What's your name?"

"Garrett – John Garrett!"

"Who sent you?"

"Miles Glub."

Father gave a grim smile. "There you are. That's all I wanted to know." He ordered the crew to shut Garrett in a cabin and guard him. In truth there was no fight left in him. He had to be carried, shivering and dripping, out of our sight.

Meg looked at my father seriously. "I thought you were really going to kill him," she said.

"So did he," said my father. "So did he!"

"Where did you learn that hateful torture?" she asked.

"From the master himself. Drake, of course. We captured a Spanish ship in the Pacific, but couldn't find an ounce of gold or silver on board. So we took the ship's clerk, a young man of about twenty-one, and asked where they had hidden it. He refused to talk. Drake put a noose around his neck, but still he wouldn't tell us the secret. So Drake dropped him into the sea with too much rope to hang him. When he pulled him out, he talked."

"Are you going to hang him when you get back to Wearmouth?" she asked.

"No. He has been hanged once and that's enough. Once

he has given evidence against Glub, I'll release him. I haven't the power to hang him anyway."

"You said you had! You said the captain of the ship had that power. Drake had when he executed Doughty."

"Drake was thousands of miles from England. We are just off the coast."

"So you lied," Meg accused him.

"Not exactly," he replied with a frown. "I said Drake had the power. I never actually said that *I* had the power."

The cabin boy approached us, holding the drum. "What shall I do with it?" he asked.

"Put it back in the sail locker," Father ordered.

Meg watched him go. "It's too late now," she said.

"What is?"

"You've beaten the drum. You don't know what it'll do now."

"The drum's got no power to do anything," I told her.

She raised one eyebrow as if to challenge me. Then she gazed over my shoulder to the coast about a mile away. I turned to see what she was looking at. The shore was quiet and deserted.

"Oh, dear," my father muttered.

"What's wrong?" I asked.

He closed his eyes and let the wind blow against his face. "The wind has turned. It's from the west. And those clouds over the land are heading this way."

"But we'll get home," I said.

"We'll have to battle against the wind. We may be facing a storm."

"It's a new ship," I said, "it can take it." I think I was trying to persuade myself that we were safe.

"Lieutenant Walsh!" my father called.

"Yes, Sir James?"

"Can we make Wearmouth before that storm hits us?"

Walsh squinted in the direction of the mass of purple cloud that had already covered the sun and was soaking us with the spray it was whipping from the wave crests. "No chance, Sir James."

"That's what I thought. We'll head close into shore and get the shelter of the cliffs until it blows over."

The men raced over the ship, fastening down and stowing away everything that was loose. We headed towards the cliffs and the shelter of Runswick Bay.

Even in the calmer water the ship was being lifted and dropped as lightly as the gulls that swam around us.

"I think your father has made a terrible mistake," said Meg.

The wind howled through the ropes and slapped them against the masts in a fury. There was no lightning in the sky, but I could hear thunder rolling. It was either thunder, or that cursed drum tormenting us.

CHAPTER SIXTEEN

"And a watery deathbed for him"

The cloud was so low that the day was dark as night. The ship's hourglass rolled off the chart table and smashed, so we had no idea of the time.

At some point, I suppose, real night fell, but all I knew was that the storm was growing worse, not better. The way we dropped down between the waves time and again was throwing my stomach into my mouth.

I'd had nothing much to eat that day yet somehow I managed to be terribly sick. After hours of suffering I thought I was going to die. After a few more hours I was wishing I *could* die.

At some time in the night my father came into the cabin. The lantern lit his face from below and threw ghastly shadows over it. "Are you ill?" I asked weakly.

"No, William, not ill. But I am worried."

"We're sinking?"

"No. This storm is nothing compared to what we went through in the Pacific. If we were in any danger, I'd use the anchor to drag the ship on to the shore and save us from drowning."

"You'd probably lose the ship," I said.

"We'll lose more than the ship, if this storm doesn't ease. Tomorrow at noon – or I should say *today* at noon

– Glub will be at Marsden Hall, waiting for his money."

"So, Drake's drum hasn't saved us. It's ruined us."

"Unless it knows of some good reason why it should keep us trapped just a few hours from home."

He lay back on his hammock. "Of course, in the end, it let down even Drake himself."

"What did happen to Drake?" I asked. "After the Armada, I mean?"

My father blew out the lantern and I lay in the darkness, listening to his voice . . .

SIR JAMES MARSDEN'S STORY

I should have stayed with Drake. After the Armada was washed away, the Queen gave orders for a fleet to destroy King Philip's remaining ships. Of course she chose Drake as one of the leaders of the expedition.

"Will there be a place for me on this trip?" I asked Drake.

He gripped my arm and looked me in the eye. "Marsden," he said. "I told you to put your money into buying land."

"I've done that."

"Then it's time you went home and looked after it. I wish I could do that. I'm getting too old and ill for all this fighting."

It was true, he was tired. Sometimes he suffered so badly from pains in his legs that he could barely walk. "England needs you," I said.

"And that's why I have to fight on. But you don't, Marsden. I'd like you to go home. Settle down. It's time you married. '*Hear the instruction of thy father, and forsake not thy mother*.' Have your parents found some young woman for you to marry?"

"No, Sir Francis," I said. The truth is I had never spent much time in the company of women. I was always more comfortable with men. Yet, since Geordie Milburn's death, I had been lonely.

"I'll arrange it," he promised. He was in London planning the expedition against Spain, yet, a week later, he had found time to talk to the Queen about my marriage. "There is a young woman who is a heroine to England," he said. "She helped trap the evil Mary Queen of Scots. It would be safer for this woman if she moved a long way away from the Catholic spies in London. Somewhere like Marsden Manor would be ideal. Her name is Marion."

"Yes, Sir Francis," I said.

So, William, I agreed to marry your mother. I first met her at our wedding – our chief guest was Sir Francis Drake. Your mother and I made a fine couple, although I was twice her age, of course. I took her back to Marsden Manor while Drake sailed off to fight the Spanish.

But Drake's luck seemed to change. Perhaps he was right to take me along as his good-luck mascot to fight the Armada. Without me the expedition against Philip went badly. A lot of men died and, worse, the Queen lost a lot of money which she had put into the scheme. She was furious. Drake wasn't punished, but he was sent back to Devon in disgrace for five years.

Still the Queen had dreams of filling her treasure chests with Spanish gold. In 1595 Drake told her there was a report of a Spanish galleon lying damaged in the Indies, just waiting to be robbed. Elizabeth and Drake couldn't resist it. She sent him with a fleet to bring back its fortune.

Drake had his own dream of capturing the treasure ports. He set off in his new ship, the *Defiance*. His spirit was as strong as ever, but everything grows weaker as it grows older. His body was sick – and even his luck seemed to have weakened over the years. Then, of course, the Spanish hadn't been idle in the twenty years since we'd raided their ships and picked them off like plums on a tree.

I was in the port at Wearmouth one day when I went into a tavern and met some sailors from the south coast. "What's the news from London?" I asked.

"Bad," one of them said. They all had long faces.

"The Spanish? A new Armada?" I asked. There had been stories that the Queen's spies were warning of a new invasion.

"No, it's Drake," one man said. He nodded to a small man in tattered breeches. "This man's just come back from the Indies."

"You sailed with Drake?" I said. "Then let me buy you a drink. I sailed with him around the world and I was with him when he fought against the Armada."

The man took the drink, but looked at me sourly. "Then I hope you had better luck than we did."

"Drake's a lucky man."

"Not any longer. The Spanish defeated us every time we met them."

"Not Drake!" I said.

"Yes, Drake. He lost us a victory in the Canary Islands because he was too slow. If we'd attacked at once, we'd have swept through the defences. By the time he'd made up his mind the Spanish were ready for us. The same in the Indies."

"Drake wasn't slow. He terrified the Spanish with the way he rushed in to the attack."

"Listen," the man snarled, "he may have done that twenty years ago, but I tell you, he was slow. The Spanish were waiting for us in every port."

"But he brought back treasure, didn't he? I still have a thousand pounds invested with him. He brought back treasure?"

"Drake brought back nothing."

"Nothing?"

"He didn't even come back. The Spanish killed some of his crew, but the sickness took more. I was serving on the *Defiance* at the time. Then Drake went down with the sickness. Some of the younger, stronger men recovered, but he was too old and weak. He went down quickly."

"He died?" I said. It was impossible to believe. Drake was not the sort of man who could ever die.

"I was on watch in the early hours of the morning, when I was ordered to fetch Drake's armour. When I took it to his cabin, I had to help him dress. He was out of bed, but his mind was fading. I asked if he thought we were going to fight. 'No,' he said. 'The Bible tells us, all men are born to die. But I want to die in my armour. I want to die like a soldier.' He was dead within the hour."

"Drake? Not Drake."

"We placed him in a lead coffin and lowered him into the sea. Trumpets played, I remember that."

"And a drum?" I said.

The man frowned. "Aye. There was a drum beating somewhere."

"There would be," I said. "He was a great man."

The sailor looked bitter. "He was a great man in the Seventies. He was some use in the Eighties. But this is the Nineties, and there's a new century coming. It belongs to new men, young men. Drake should have died twenty years ago. Then my friends wouldn't be dead now."

I understood. "You lost friends to the disease?" I said. "Yes. That happened to me too. I'm sorry. I know how you feel."

I left him to his drinking and went home to mourn Drake alone. Not the Drake that the sailor knew, the Drake that I used to know. He was like a knight of olden times, my Drake. But a knight of the sea. He sailed by the stars and was master of the storms.

But everything passes, William. All men are born to die. I just hope he is resting in heaven. The Spanish will swear forever that he was the Devil himself with a devil's heart and his devil drum.

My father went quiet, lost in his own thoughts and memories. I'm not sure if, in the end, he was talking to me or to himself.

I fell into an exhausted sleep and woke to find the ship rolling, but not being thrown about so badly.

My father had left his hammock and I dressed quickly. He was on deck inspecting the ship and making her ready to sail. It was dark, but the sky was showing the first signs of dawn. "No great damage," he said. "The sea is still heavy, but we'll have to risk it if we're going to get back to Marsden Hall for noon."

Meg brought me some cheese and I was surprised to find I had an appetite. "Will we get back in time?" she asked.

"It's hard to tell. It depends on your magic drum."

The wind wasn't in the best direction, but we watched the headlands and bays of North Yorkshire give way to the coastline of Durham and our spirits began to rise. At Wearmouth the crew had to climb into the ship's boat and row us up the river to our mooring.

The cobbled quayside was glistening, washed clean by the storm. I ran to the gangplank. "Right foot first!" my father cried. He was too late. Meg and I raced across to the tavern to collect our horses. "What time is it?" I asked the taverner.

"Almost half-past eleven."

"Half an hour to get back to Marsden Hall," I said.

"Without the money," said Meg.

We led three horses to the ship and found my father standing there, surrounded by a group of men. "We've half an hour!" I called to him.

He walked over to me and said, "I am selling the cargo," he said.

"It won't make enough money," I said.

"You're wrong!" he cried. "It's some sort of miracle! Last night's storm has ruined the corn harvest in the north. Whole fields are flattened and the grain will rot on the ground. These corn dealers are willing to offer anything to get our cargo of grain."

"A thousand pounds?"

"They're up to seven hundred," Father said.

"But you can't wait for them to hold an auction," Meg said urgently.

"I have to. You two ride for Marsden Hall now and keep Glub there till I arrive with the money. It may take a while for the dealer to get that amount of cash, of course. But I'll be there."

He turned back to the dealers while Meg and I mounted the horses and headed for home.

All along the river bank there were sailors looking at the damage to their ships. Hulls had been split where the gales had torn away moorings and driven ships into each other. Masts lay snapped in a tangle of rigging and cabins were crushed by falling spars.

The road to Marsden village was flooded and in places the horses were wading past their knees in muddy water. The fields were a pitiful sight with the corn, ready for harvesting, lying flat and sodden. Sheep looked at us mournfully as they stood on islands in flooded fields, and trees dripped streams of water on to us.

When the midday sun came out, the roads began to steam, shrouding the land in a thin mist that deadened any sounds around us. All we could hear was the splashing of our horses on the path. The bridge at Fatfield was only just above the level of the flood water. As we crossed it, the tower of Marsden Hall rose out of the mist.

"Nearly home," I urged Meg.

"Home?" she said. "But for how much longer?"

CHAPTER SEVENTEEN

"You are welcome home, my Lord"

Our welcome home was like a funeral.

We had thrown our horses' reins to Martin the Ostler and run across to the entrance from the courtyard. The house seemed to be deserted, yet, as we rushed into the main hall, we found the family were all there.

It was too warm for a fire, so the grate lay black and cold. Mother sat in her chair with embroidery on her knee, but her hands were not working at it. Grandfather and Grandmother sat grey-faced and still, while Great-Uncle George stood by the window, his hand tapping at the sword he always wore at his belt.

Sitting at the table by the window was Miles Glub. His bald head was streaked with sweat and his twisted mouth was turned up in a happy smile. It vanished as we walked through the door.

"Is Sir James with you?" my mother asked.

"He's following."

"Does he have the money?" Grandfather asked anxiously.

"He will have," Meg promised.

The old man rested a hand on Grandmother's shoulder and squeezed it. "So the journey went well?"

"Apart from an attack by some villains off the coast of Yorkshire," I said, looking at Glub.

"No one is safe these days," said Glub smoothly. "Not even Sir James Marsden. It is shameful the way these pirates are allowed to get away with it."

"But they haven't got away with it," I said. "We captured a man called John Garrett. We can hang him as an example to the others," I went on carefully, "or we can let him go if he promises to tell us who put him up to it."

"Garrett is a man as hard as Spanish steel . . . at least that's what I've heard. He has a reputation in Newcastle for being unbeaten in a fight with any man."

"But he *has* been beaten in a fight with a barrel of rotten fish," Meg said.

Glub pushed himself up from the table. "Jumping on board a ship is no great crime. It's not so bad as marooning a fellow traveller, is it?" he demanded.

"Who was marooned?"

"*I* was!" Glub said and his squeaking voice rose higher. "Your father waited till I left the ship in London, then sailed off without me. I was penniless in a strange city. I could have died. I will not forget that, Master Marsden. The good Sir James thinks that, because he is a gentleman, he can treat men like me in any way he wants. Well, I'm going to show him he can't."

"What are you planning?"

"Planning? Why, I'm planning to take Marsden Hall from you and your ancient family."

"But Father has the money."

"I don't *want* the money. I want to see you out of this house. You had better start packing, because from noon this house belongs to me." His gaze swept round the room. "Do you understand?"

"You can't refuse to take the money," Great-Uncle George said angrily.

"Oh, but I can." He pulled a sheet of parchment from inside his grubby waistcoat and slapped it on the table. "If my money is not paid by noon on this day, then I take Marsden Hall."

There was the faint sound of a bell ringing in the distance. "What's that?"

"The clock at the church tower," Grandfather said wearily.

"And what is it striking?"

"Noon," Grandmother said.

"Then Marsden Manor is mine!" the man crowed. "You have five minutes to get out of here, or I will call the local constable and have you thrown out! Get out! Get out!" His pink face was turning purple and his linen shirt was stained with sweat from his massive body.

The family started slowly to move, but Meg crossed the room and said, "Can I see the document?"

"You can't even read it, girl," Glub sneered.

Meg took the deed from the table and frowned as she tried to make out the words. "It's like *The Merchant of Venice*," she said quietly.

"What's that?" Glub asked.

"A play. A jealous man refused to take the money he was owed. He preferred to take his *revenge*."

"And I don't blame him!" Glub laughed.

"The family pleaded with him," Meg explained.

"Plead away!" Glub cried. "I'd enjoy that."

"They even offered him more than they owed."

"It wouldn't work. You can't put a price on the pleasure of *revenge*."

"But in the end he never got his *revenge*," said Meg.

"What?" said Glub.

"The moneylender had been careless about the deed,"

Meg explained. "He was so eager to destroy his enemy that he was careless. But the law isn't careless. The law has to be obeyed to the letter."

Glub snatched the document from her. "And it says I receive one thousand pounds before noon today, or I take Marsden Hall."

The family stood quietly, watching Meg, who was moving around the room like the boy who had acted Portia on the stage. She was beginning to enjoy her role and remember the play. "It says here that you may take the hall at Marsden, so take it."

"I mean to."

"Of course, you'll starve."

Glub narrowed his eyes. "Why?"

"Because you are *in* the hall of Marsden," Meg said. "But you can't get out, can you?"

"Yes!" Glub exploded impatiently. "I simply walk through that door into the passage."

"No!" Meg said sharply. "Sir George!" she said to my great-uncle. "Guard that door. This man is not allowed to leave."

Now Glub's enjoyment of the scene was fading and he was growing angry. He could swat Meg out of his way like a cook swats a fly. I had my knife at my belt, but I wasn't sure that would stop him if he turned violent. Great-Uncle George's sword was another matter. It was a heavy old thing, but I knew from our practices that he still used it well.

The old knight didn't understand what Meg was doing, but he marched over to the door as she'd asked, drew his sword and faced Glub.

"Get out of my house!" Glub cried.

"It's not your house," Meg said.

"It is! The deed says so."

"No. The deed says you own the '*hall*'. If it had a capital letter at the start of 'hall' you might have had a case. But some careless clerk gave it a small 'h'. You are in the '*hall*'. But the only way out is through the door, or through the window. You are too fat to get through the window, Master Glub, so that only leaves the door."

"Then I'll use the door."

"But once you step outside the door you are in the house. And the house is still owned by the Marsden family. You only own the *hall*."

"That's not what it means!" Glub wailed.

"But that's what it *says*!" Meg answered. She turned to Grandfather. "You were magistrate for years before Sir James took over. You know the law. Am I right?"

Grandfather straightened his back and looked stern. "You are right," he said.

"And does Miles Glub have your permission to step into your passage outside?"

"He does not."

"And if he stepped into the passage without your permission, would he be breaking the law?"

"He would be trespassing."

"And what would Sir George do if he saw someone trespassing?"

The old knight had a wide grin that showed under his thick white beard. "I would probably chop him into little pieces and feed him to the geese!" He waved the sword in Glub's direction.

"Keep away from me with that sword!" the man screeched.

"Sir George doesn't need to come near you with the sword," said Meg. "You will die within a few days if you don't get water. Maybe two days in warm weather like this. You can't get out to get water. And the Marsden family may not let anyone bring you a cup."

"That's murder!"

"Not really," Grandfather said. "After all, you walked into this room of your own free will. We didn't drag you in and imprison you."

"No, but you could let me out!"

"I can't give you permission to leave," the old man said.

"Why not?"

"Because it isn't my room any longer. It's owned by some fat fellow from Newcastle. What's his name again, Meg?"

"Grub?"

"Or maybe Grab," chuckled Grandmother.

"You can't do this to me!" sobbed Glub.

"Do what?" asked my father as he opened the door and stepped into the room.

"Sir James! Your family have threatened to starve me to death. I'm their prisoner and they won't let me go!" said Glub.

"Really?" my father said blinking. The idea of three old people and two very young ones holding a powerful man like Glub in an open room was ridiculous. "I thought you'd be glad to take the thousand pounds and go!" He held up a leather saddle pack heavy with coins.

"Oh, yes, I am!" Glub cried, reaching for the bag.

"Wait!" I said. "Remember the play, Meg? The moneylender had to buy his freedom. How much should we charge Master Glub?"

"What?" Glub asked.

I explained. "You told us you didn't want the money, you wanted the hall. You took it – so we don't owe you a penny."

"Yes, but . . ."

"Unless you want to sell the hall, of course."

Glub's frightened face cleared. "Ah! I see! Yes! I sell the hall back to the family for the thousand pounds it cost me."

"Not exactly," I said. "You sell the hall for whatever you can get."

"It's worth a thousand pounds."

"One pound."

"What?"

"One pound." I reached into my father's saddle pack and took out one golden sovereign. "Take one pound. Tear up that deed and you are free to go."

Glub's eyes rolled wildly. "That's not fair."

"What was it you said, Master Glub? You can't put a price on the pleasure of *revenge*. Well, it will cost us one sovereign. I think it's a bargain, don't you?"

A mixture of sweat and tears ran down his pink cheeks. "You're just like your father," he said softly.

He took the gold sovereign from my hand, tore up the deed and let the pieces fall to the floor. Then he walked towards the door, his head hanging. Great-Uncle George lowered the sword to let him pass.

"You aren't really going to let the poor man go without his money, are you?" my mother asked.

"We can't," Meg agreed.

My father sighed. "On my honour as a gentleman, I can't," he admitted.

"I agree," Grandmother said.

"I suppose we have to pay the man," Grandfather nodded.

"If you must," Great-Uncle George said with a sigh.

Father raised the saddle pack and handed it to Glub.

The man looked around the family. "Marsden Hall

must mean a lot to you," he said. He turned and walked slowly out of the room.

"If you'd sent him away without a penny he'd have understood," Meg said quietly to me. "Now he's in your debt he'll never forgive you."

My father took off his mud-spattered riding cloak and shook his head. "I'm not quite sure what that was all about," he admitted. "How did you manage to terrify that bully of a man?"

My mother gave a wide smile and said, "Welcome home, James. Sit down and tell us about your journey."

Chapter Eighteen

"I pray you, give me leave to go from here"

The summer grew hotter and some of the crops in the fields recovered. The harvest would not be such a disaster this year after all. More Marsden coal went to London and the fortunes of the Marsden family recovered. We talked about having another ship built. Father said, "*Revenge II* might be a good name."

"After Drake's Armada ship?"

"And to remind us of the pleasures that 'revenge' can bring," he said. My father had made his first joke!

I had to work hard to help my father with his accounts that summer. He was still not an easy man to love, but at least we were starting to understand one another. The journey to Plymouth had done that much.

In the heat of the short summer nights I often lay awake for hours with my waking dreams; dreams of Stratford and the Globe Theatre. But, most of all, I was planning what I could say to my father. How could I tell him I wanted to leave?

One night, when the hot air was as still as the stones of Marsden Hall, I heard the rattle. The soft beating of the drum. Since we had brought it from the *Hawk*, it had lain in a cupboard on the landing.

I slipped out of my bed, threw on a robe and walked

barefoot down the midnight corridor. The sound was not coming from the corridor, but from a room next to my mother's. This was the room Meg had moved into when she became my mother's maidservant. Now the yellow glow of a candle spilled out from under the door and with it the soft drumming.

I turned the door handle slowly. Meg sat on her bed, fully clothed. The drum was on the bed in front of her. She looked up with her sea-green eyes wide and wondering.

"You were playing the drum?" I said. "Why?"

"No," she said, "it was playing itself. It's restless. It wants to go home."

"Where is home?"

"Buckland Abbey. It doesn't belong to us."

"It doesn't," my father agreed. He was standing behind me in the doorway.

"Everything has its place," Meg said. "The Marsdens have Marsden Hall. And there's a special kind of magic that made sure you didn't lose it. The drum has its place, just as much as you do."

"Is that witchcraft?" I asked.

"No," she said, "it's just something old Jane Atkinson told me. She's the wisest woman in the whole county. It's magic – but it isn't witchcraft."

My father sat on the edge of Meg's bed and touched the drum. "We are all drawn to the place where our true spirit lies," he agreed. "Even a drum."

"And your place is Marsden Hall?" I said.

He looked at me. "No, William. This summer I have discovered that my place is at sea. The *Hawk* is just a simple collier to most people, but she is a part of me, the way a close friend becomes part of you."

"Like Mother?" I asked.

"No. I was thinking of Geordie Milburn," he said. "That was a dangerous journey to Plymouth, with pirates and storms and a race against the hourglass of time. But I have never felt so alive since I sailed with Drake."

"So, your place is the sea?" I asked.

"I think so. I think I will make more journeys with the *Hawk*. Maybe our next ship will sail across to Flanders or France or the Mediterranean! But first I have to go back to Plymouth. I have to take Drake's drum home. I have a feeling it still has important work to do."

I hardly dared breathe my question. "Where is *my* home?"

Father pulled at his thin beard and thought about it. "Where have you *felt* most at home?"

"On the stage of the Globe with Master Shakespeare's acting company," I said.

"Then that's where you have to go," Father said.

After telling me for two years that he would never let me go, this was too sudden for me to take in. "Really?"

He nodded. "I did not really learn about life till I was forced to sail off with Captain Drake. Your Master Shakespeare may not be so great a man as Drake, of course."

"He is!" said Meg. "Why, it was Master Shakespeare's clever play that saved Marsden Hall from Miles Glub!"

"I learned everything from my two great friends, Captain Milburn and Captain Drake," my father went on. "If you can learn half as much from Master Shakespeare, you will be a lucky young man."

"So, I can go to join him?"

"I will take you to London myself," he promised. "On the next trip."

I wanted to throw an arm around him and hug him. But

that was something I had never done and maybe never would. "Thank you," I said.

He gave a tight smile, looked embarrassed at even those two words and hurried from the room. I looked at Meg and she looked back at me. "It's the magic of the drum," she said.

"Perhaps."

I rose and began to follow my father out of the door. I stopped when I had a sudden thought. "So, Father's place is at sea, and mine is with the theatre company, and the drum's is at Buckland."

"Yes."

"So where is your place?"

"That would be telling," she said.

"But you know?"

"I know."

"Is it at Marsden Hall?"

"Sometimes," she said.

I didn't understand. Not then.

Later.

The road by the River Wear looks different when you are riding *away* from the house. That bright September morning, with the dew heavy on the grass, I felt a confused mixture of sadness and excitement.

I'd said goodbye to my mother at the gate. She'd been as calm as ever, but my grandfather was troubled. He stood next to Grandmother and Great-Uncle George. "I remember saying goodbye to your father when he sailed off twenty-five years ago," he said.

"He came back," I said cheerfully, "and I'll come back."

"That was twenty-five years ago," Grandfather said,

"when your father left."

"Be quiet, you old fool," Grandmother snapped. "You'll upset the boy."

It was as I reached Fatfield Bridge that I realized what Grandfather was trying to say. "They're getting old," I said to Meg, who was riding with us.

She didn't reply.

"They – they may not all be here when I get back. What was it Drake said before he died? All men are born to die?"

I turned before we reached the end of the bridge. I knew it was the last chance I'd have to see the top of the towers. My last view of Marsden Manor.

"You'll see it again," Meg said.

"But I'll be a man then, not a boy."

I rode on and didn't look back.

We loaded our saddle packs on to the *Hawk*. The crew were so pleased to see us it warmed my aching heart. "We've got your net all ready for you, Master William, in case we're attacked," Master Walsh laughed.

"He even went and bought a barrel of rotten fish for you, Miss Meg."

"Meg won't be coming with us," I said quickly. "She's only here to wave us goodbye."

The men looked a little disappointed, but Meg was calm and eager to talk to everyone. Drake's drum was the last thing to be carried on board. The men looked at it with respect and it was given a place of honour in the captain's cabin.

"Tide's on the turn, Captain Marsden!" Master Walsh called.

"Then let's get under way," my father said, leaning on the rail next to Meg.

"Meg hasn't left yet!" I cried.

He ignored me. "Raise the gangplank!" he cried.

"You'll have to hurry!" I told her.

She tilted her head to one side and looked at me curiously. "You, and your father, and the drum are all going where you belong. I'm going where *I* belong," she said.

"You didn't tell me where that was."

She turned her face to the sun and closed her eyes. "There's something your mother read to me from her Bible. Sir Francis Drake would have liked it. It was about a woman called Ruth. She'd lost her family, just like me. So she adopted a new family, and she said, 'Ask me not to leave you, or to return from following after you. For where *you* go, *I* will go; and where *you* live, *I* will live; your people shall be my people.'"

I knew that Bible story. When her new family saw how determined Ruth was, they gave up trying to argue. It was as little use to argue with Meg Lumley.

She opened her eyes and looked at me. "Sorry, Will, but I think I know where I belong."

The ship drifted slowly down the river like the sand in the hourglass.

The Historical Characters

The Marsden family are fictional, but the main events of the story are true and so are several of the characters:

SIR FRANCIS DRAKE (1540 – 1596) A great navigator and explorer – although some prefer to call him a great pirate. He learned sailing skills from a shipowner in his native Devon. He inherited the ship and decided he wanted to see more of the world. He began to make his fortune from trading across the Atlantic Ocean and, if the trade was in slaves, then he wasn't too bothered. In 1577 he was given a secret task by Elizabeth I to raid the Spanish colonies in the Pacific. Not only did he collect a fortune for his queen (and himself), but he became the first Englishman to take a ship all the way around the world. He helped defeat the Spanish Armada in 1588, when he wasn't helping himself to Spanish treasure. The Spanish called him '*El Draque*' – the Dragon – and swore he was in partnership with the Devil. Drake's later expeditions against the Spanish were a failure and he died in 1596, trying to relive the great raiding days of his 1577 adventure.

QUEEN ELIZABETH I (1533 – 1603) The Queen did not want war with Spain, but she was tempted by the riches the Spanish were bringing back from America. From time to time, Elizabeth's own English sailors had her permission to steal from the Spanish treasure ships. She gave them a licence and they called themselves "privateers" (although in fact they were little better than pirates). When her "privateers" returned with a fortune, she took a huge share and rewarded men like Drake with a knighthood. But she did not like her privateers to fail and, when they lost her money, she was furious. Elizabeth was a bad loser.

WILLIAM SHAKESPEARE (1564 – 1616) Shakespeare travelled to London to become an actor, but quickly became a popular playwright. Then he discovered that he could make more money by owning part of his theatre. He was one of the owners of the Globe Theatre. Queen Elizabeth supported his theatre companies and he became quite wealthy. But even the Queen couldn't keep his theatre open when attacks of plague swept through London in the summer months. At those times he would return to his home in Stratford to visit the wife and family he had left there.

THOMAS DOUGHTY (15–[?]–1578) A gentleman who put money into Drake's 1577 expedition. In return he expected a share of the treasure that Drake found. To make sure his money was safe, he went along on the voyage to keep an eye on Drake. It is likely that he upset Drake by trying to interfere with the captain's plans. It's certain he didn't get along with Drake – Doughty was rather a snob and thought Drake "common". Drake took his revenge by claiming that Doughty was a traitor who was stirring the men up to a mutiny – he could have been right. Drake took swift action to stop Doughty making trouble by having him beheaded.

DRAKE'S DRUM Drake took an old drum with him on his journey around the world. There is nothing to say that Drake thought it was special, but in later years Drake's drum gained its own legend. Some people say the drum sounds as a warning whenever England is in danger, or that it should be beaten if the country is threatened by another Armada. When Drake hears the drum he will rise from his watery grave and come back to lead his country to safety. Many people have claimed they heard the drum in wartime. It was last heard during World War II when German bombers began the Battle of Britain. The drum still exists and can be seen at Drake's old home, Buckland Abbey near Plymouth.

THE GOLDEN HINDE The Elizabethans tried to protect the famous ship and kept her in dry dock on the Thames. But the wood rotted till she was just a skeleton and, less than eighty years after she'd sailed around the world, she was broken into fragments. Some were used to make a chair that is now in the Bodleian Library in Oxford.

The Time Trail

1492 Christopher Columbus discovers a "New World" across the Atlantic. He claims it for the Catholic Kings of Spain, who paid for his voyage.

1493 Spain and Portugal divide up the "New World", South America, between them. It promises to become a treasure chest of precious stones and metals.

1522 A Spanish ship becomes the first vessel ever to sail around the world. Of the 265 men who set off, only 15 come back. The Portuguese captain, Magellan, dies in a fight with natives in the Philippines in 1521.

1540(?) Francis Drake born in Devon, England.

1553 King Edward VI of England dies and his sister, Mary Tudor, takes the thone. Under Edward, England had followed the Protestant religion. Mary tries to take the country back to being Catholic.

1554 Queen Mary marries her cousin, the Catholic Philip II of Spain. Of course he sees himself as King of England. The English people disagree.

1558 When Mary dies, the throne goes to her Protestant sister, Elizabeth. She refuses to marry Philip II of Spain. He begins to plot to take the throne from her. English and Spanish hatred grows over the next forty years, even though they are rarely at war.

1568 England and Spain come close to war when English privateers steal Spanish gold and silver. The money is a great help to Elizabeth.

1572–3 Francis Drake makes a fortune for Elizabeth with raids on Spanish colonies in America. Elizabeth is trying to make peace with Spain and is not too pleased.

1580 Drake arrives back in England after sailing around the world. Only the second crew to do this and the first English. Queen Elizabeth rewards him by making him Sir Francis. Since he stole a lot of Spanish treasure on his voyage, the Spanish are furious and begin to plot revenge.

1587 The Spanish support a plot to put the Catholic Mary Queen of Scots on the English throne. But, before they can send an army to help, Elizabeth has Mary executed.

1588 The Spanish invasion force, the Armada, finally arrives. The English navy, led by Lord Howard, do little damage. Sir Francis Drake does capture a storm-wrecked Spanish ship and takes a lot of treasure from her. Storms drive the Armada away from England and save England from an invasion.

1589 Elizabeth sends Drake to Spain to finish off the remains of the Armada. He fails, a lot of men die and Elizabeth loses the £20,000 she spent on the expedition. Drake returns to Devon in disgrace.

1595 Drake sets off on another raiding expedition against the Spanish colonies in America. The Spanish towns are better defended now and Drake fails.

1596 Drake catches the fever that has been killing many of his crew. He calls for his armour so that he can die like a soldier. He is buried at sea.

1598 Philip of Spain dies, and the danger of another Spanish war dies with him. Elizabeth has outlived her last great rival.

1603 Elizabeth dies. She has no children and is the last of the Tudors. James VI of Scotland takes the English throne.

Also in the *Tudor Chronicles* series

The Prince of Rags and Patches

A visitor comes to Marsden Manor, bearing a letter from the dying Queen Elizabeth to James VI of Scotland.

A man lies dead in Bournmoor Woods – murdered.

And Will Marsden, aided and abetted by Meg the serving girl, sets out to find the killer.

Meanwhile Will is puzzling over the story of his Marsden ancestor who followed Richard III into battle, was mixed up in the mysterious deaths of the Princes in the Tower . . . and whose meeting with a prince of rags and patches gives Will the clue he needs.

Two parallel stories of murder and intrigue,
each building to a thrilling climax!

The King in Blood Red and Gold

When handsome, foppish Hugh Richmond turns up at Marsden Manor, claiming to be one of Queen Elizabeth's spies and asking for help, Will and his grandfather seize on the chance for adventure!

Riding north to Scotland, Grandfather tells Will he fought

at the Battle of Flodden Field in the service of Henry VIII. Then as now, there were desperate skirmishes on the Borders between the English and the Scots Reivers – cattle thieves.

Neither of them realize quite what danger Hugh is leading them into and it seems that all their courage and quick wit will not get them out.

Luckily, Meg the serving girl is very clever . . .

Two interwoven stories of battle and adventure,
each as exciting as the other.

The Lady of Fire and Tears

A silver cup has been stolen from Marsden Hall and Meg the serving girl will hang for it. Unless she agrees to spy on her friends at the Black Bull Tavern . . .

For loyal Meg it is a terrible dilemma. Her friend Will is desperate to save her. And Will's mother decides to tell them a story she has kept secret for many years . . . how she herself, as a young lady-in-waiting, was forced to spy on Mary, Queen of Scors.

Next in the *Tudor Chronicles* series

The Lord of the Dreaming Globe (June 2006)
The Queen of the Dying Light (June 2006)